"I've never forced a woman," Bart said

"Whatever happens between us will be because we both want it."

"That wasn't the impression I got on the way down here," Melissa replied carefully, settling herself on the lounger.

He swung around to face her. "That was a joke that misfired," he confessed. "I was coming on business anyway and thought you might find it fun to tag along. I was going to tell you on the plane, but when you got angry I decided to keep quiet and play along with it."

"You mean all that guff about wanting me was a lie, too?" she asked, looking at him beneath lowered lids.

"Of course not." Bart spoke with quiet vehemence. "But I didn't bring you here to force myself on you. I just thought that away from Rick and his influence, I might stand a chance of making you fall for me."

Kay Clifford is a British writer whose books have appeared in the Harlequin Romance line in the past few years. Readers will welcome her newest lightly sophisticated romance.

Books by Kay Clifford

HARLEQUIN ROMANCE

Dream of Love
Kay Clifford

Harlequin Books

TORONTO • NEW YORK • LONDON
AMSTERDAM • PARIS • SYDNEY • HAMBURG
STOCKHOLM • ATHENS • TOKYO • MILAN

Original hardcover edition published in 1987
by Mills & Boon Limited

ISBN 0-373-02881-4

Harlequin Romance first edition January 1988

CHAPTER ONE

Melissa Abbot looked up from her word processor as her employer came into the room. Tall and broad-shouldered, and bronzed from his recent African safari, he gave her the smile that had his women fans swooning at his feet.

'I thought you were leaving early,' he said.

'I was waiting for you to sign the cheque for your ex-wife.'

With a sigh, Richard Rayburn picked up his pen and watching him, Melissa appreciated why it infuriated him to do so. His ex-wife, Jessica Welles, was an American film actress as famous as he, and had no need of the high alimony he had to pay her until, and if, she re-married.

'I wish I'd never agreed to do another film with her,' he muttered, sliding the signed cheque across the desk. 'When I think of seeing her on the set every day, I get another grey hair.'

Melissa grinned at the absurdity of the comment, for Richard Rayburn's luxuriant black hair, perfect profile and flat stomach, were a cameraman's dream, needing so little in the way of make-up and lighting to enhance him that his claim to be thirty-nine when he was actually ten years older was accepted without question.

'I wouldn't worry about grey hairs, Mr

Rayburn,' she soothed. 'When it's white as snow, you'll still be playing the hero.'

Although used to compliments, he looked pleased. Perhaps because he rarely got one from her.

'Nervous about tonight?' he asked, accompanying her into the hall of his apartment.

'Petrified,' Melissa admitted, knowing that three hours from now she'd be on stage in the Maida Vale church hall, playing Blanche in 'A Streetcar Named Desire'. 'I don't know why I ever imagined amateur dramatics would be fun! I'm sick with nerves!'

'Then I won't offer you a part in my next film,' he teased.

Laughing at the very thought, Melissa said goodnight to him and walked into the lift, realising for the umpteenth time how lucky she was to have this job, for, despite being a star, her employer was the easiest man to work for.

Publicised as 'macho', he was rarely seen without a pretty girl on each arm. Yet Melissa was grateful he had never made a pass at *her*, for a rejection might have spoiled their camaraderie, which was something she valued much more than the generous salary he paid her.

But then she was in the unique position of being heiress to a considerable fortune, though only a few well-trusted people knew of it: one was her best friend Katy, whose parents, Ruth and Martin Berger, had taken Melissa under their wing and into their home when her mother and father had been killed in an avalanche when she was thirteen.

Legally she had been the ward of two eccentric

bachelor uncles who lived in splendid isolation on an island off the coast of Scotland, but they had willingly allowed her to live with the Bergers, content to get monthly letters from her, to which they replied with a card at Christmas.

With a gift for languages, she had elected to become a bilingual secretary after leaving school, and had landed the job with Richard Rayburn when he'd been filming in France and his own secretary had left to get married. She could not envisage working for anyone else, and wasn't sure she'd bother getting a temporary job while he was filming in Hollywood.

She would have liked to go with him, if only to meet his ex-wife, Jessica, for she had often wondered what special quality the woman had to have caught him. Perhaps it was her social register background, so different from his own, as the son of a London bus conductor. Not that he was ashamed of his origins. On the contrary, he was proud of them.

Occasionally he'd questioned Melissa about her own past, but she had remained evasive.

'Beats me why you feel guilty about your money,' Katy had espostulated only last week. 'I'm not suggesting you be like Christina Onassis, but you could at least give up work for a year and have a good time.'

'I have a good time working,' Melissa had smiled.

'Okay, but at least stop pretending you need to work for a living! It'll lead you to trouble one day!'

Of course her friend was right, for Melissa knew her day of reckoning would come when she met the man she wanted to marry. In the circle in which she moved, she was unlikely to meet anyone as well-heeled as herself, and she couldn't imagine how the man in question would react to the news that she could afford to keep him in a manner to which he was entirely unaccustomed!

Inexplicably, this crossed her mind a few hours later while she was changing into her costume in the backstage room. Perhaps it was because Tony Goodsall, her co-star and current boy-friend, was showing signs that his interest in her was more than casual. Trouble was she didn't regard him as anything but a friend, so being truthful about her background didn't come into it. But one day it could be a problem.

'Fifteen minutes to curtain up,' a voice called, and she hurriedly began applying her stage make-up.

Below average height and slenderly built, she had an innocent air that contrasted with her practical nature. Her soft voice was deceptive too, masking determination and a tongue that at times could be sharp. Her red-gold hair was her giveaway, for its rich lustre lit up the dingy room as, released from its usual topknot, it rippled to her shoulders like a fall of autumn leaves.

Despite its dramatic colour, it was her eyes that held the attention. Large and aquamarine, they were fringed by long lashes several shades darker than her hair, and changed colour with her mood: blue as the Mediterranean when she was happy, paling to slate when she was not. The rest of her features were good too: a small straight nose with a smattering of freckles, a wide, generous mouth with a full lower lip, and a rounded yet determinded chin.

Another call sent her hurrying to the side of the stage, and, hearing her cue, she moved into the spotlight.

The first act passed without a hitch, and as the curtain came down to applause, Tony Goodsall gave her a hug.

'Looks like we've made it,' he said. 'You were terrific, Melissa. If we——'

He stopped mid-sentence, distracted by chairs scraping back in the auditorium. Going across to the curtain, he peeped through.

'Well, that's a turn-up for the book,' he muttered. 'Your boss has just walked in. Why didn't you tell us he was coming?'

'I didn't know.' Melissa joined Tony at the curtain, and saw Richard Rayburn—seemingly oblivious to the sensation his presence was causing—casually chatting to Katy and her parents.

'I suppose his current girl-friend let him down,' she muttered, 'and he didn't fancy being alone.'

Her supposition proved correct, for he said so when he came backstage to congratulate her after the performance.

'And I'm glad she did,' he added, 'or I wouldn't have seen you tonight. You're a good actress, Melissa. Ever considered taking it up professionally?'

'Perish the idea!' she said, and was stopped from saying more by being immediately surrounded by the other members of the cast who could not believe their luck in seeing the famous Rick Rayburn at first hand.

He even joined them at the party Tony gave

in his apartment, but when Rick offered to see Melissa and Katy home afterwards, Melissa prettily refused, not wishing to change the tenor of their relationship.

'You could have him as a boy-friend,' Katy remarked as they undressed for bed.

'I prefer him as my boss.'

'Struck on Tony, then?'

'You know I'm not. In fact he's making noises about introducing me to his parents, which is the last thing I need.'

'Then you'd better make it clearer to him,' Katy said bluntly. 'He was watching you like a love-sick calf tonight.'

Oh, lord! Melissa thought, and determined to take her friend's advice.

Next morning Rick's news drove Tony and everyone else from her mind.

'My agent phoned me from Los Angeles at half-past four this morning,' he grumbled, 'and ruined what was left of the night.'

'Don't tell me the film deal's off!'

'Nothing like that,' came the reply. 'He called to say I've been invited to stay at the home of the guy who's putting up the money for the movie.'

'Why should that upset you? It'll be nicer than living in a hotel for weeks on end.'

'It would be—if he hadn't invited my ex-wife too! Can you imagine Jessica and me under the same roof?'

'No, I can't,'

'But I daren't turn down the invitation,' the star went on, running his fingers through his glossy hair. 'Mr Moneybags insists the only way he can stay within the budget is to have the two of us where he can keep an eye on us.'

Melissa undersood why, for the actress had a reputation for lateness and tantrums—her temper even causing co-stars and directors to walk off the set. It was only her popularity at the box office that kept her working, and she frequently took advantage of this popularity by making herself as disagreeable as possible.

'Why don't you call Mr Moneybags?' Melissa suggested, 'and tell him how you feel about Jessica.'

'He knows,' Rick grated. 'That's why he wants us living with him—so he can make sure we don't get at each other's throats. I'll have to agree, I'm afraid, or he'll withdrawn his finance.'

'Oh!'

'Exactly,' the star growled. 'And this is too good a film for me to back out of. So I've decided I must take a girl along with me.'

'A girl?'

'Sure. I can't spend weeks under the same roof as Jessica without a girl on my arm, otherwise she'll be after me like a shot!'

'I thought you two couldn't stand each other.'

'Out of bed, we can't,' he said frankly. 'But in bed, she's the greatest. So if I don't have someone in tow, she'll try to seduce me—simply to satisfy her ego.' He shook his head wryly. 'She's never forgiven me for walking out on her.'

'Understandable,' Melissa concurred. 'So who will you take with you?'

'None of my current girl-friends will do,' Rick Rayburn replied. 'They're good-looking enough, but not classy. Actually I'd like Jessica to think

I'm getting married again, so the girl I take has to look and act as if she could be my future wife.'

'You might have to employ an actress to play the part.'

'Not a bad idea,' Rick frowned. 'Except, what guarantee do I have she'll keep her mouth shut afterwards? I could look a right fool if she sells her story to the press. No, Melissa. I need someone I can trust, someone beautiful, ladylike and——' Abruptly he stopped speaking, and equally abruptly his frown vanished. 'I've got it! The perfect solution.'

'What is?'

'*You*,' he answered, giving her the winsome smile that melted the heart of millions, but had little effect on Melissa. She was too used to seeing him use it to get his own way.

'You're classy, pretty and, after watching you on stage last night, I know you can act.'

'But not well enough to be your girl-friend,' Melissa said firmly.

'All you'll have to do is look at me adoringly, and be affectionate when anyone's around. I'll make it worth your while, Melissa. I'll give you enough money to buy a complete new wardrobe, and a big fat bonus as well.' He leaned across her desk and caught her hand. 'Please, angel, help me out.'

Melissa was in a quandary—not wanting to get personally involved with her employer, yet appreciating his problem. She knew his fear of being ensnared again by his ex-wife was genuine, for, despite his self-confident façade, underneath he was emotionally uncertain of himself.

'You've got nothing to lose,' Rick went on.

'We'll be wined and dined by all the big names in Hollywood, and you'll be living in luxury like a princess . . .'

Still Melissa hesitated. It would be fun testing her acting skill in real-life role, fun too to get an inside view of Hollywood. But it could also give Rick the wrong idea about her, and lead to complications.

'You're wrong,' he said, reading her thoughts. 'If you think I've carnal designs on you, forget it. I look on you almost as a daught——' he caught himself in time '—sister,' he corrected, 'and I'll behave just like a brother—even when I have to kiss you!'

Melissa hid a smile at his slip of the tongue. Even with her, he preserved the mask of youth.

'I mean it,' Rick insisted. 'So how about saying yes?'

'Very well,' she said slowly. 'But if you make *one* pass at me, I'll leave you flat.'

'We'll only put on an act in public and whenever Jessica's around,' he assured her. 'Now give me my cheque book. I want you to buy yourself a whole new wardrobe. You not only have to act my girl-friend, you have to look the part too.'

She nodded and took the cheque from him, surprised to see the amount on it.

'Nothing's too good for my girl!' he smiled, seeing her expression. 'So go and spend the lot.'

Later that evening, telling Katy about it, Melissa almost changed her mind.

'You'd be crazy not to go with him,' Katy argued.

'What if he makes a pass at me? I know he says he won't, but . . .'

'Hundreds of girls would be delighted to change places with you.'

'Would *you* be?'

'I might.'

'Who are you kidding?' Melissa snorted. 'We both always said we want more from a relationship than sex.'

Katy sighed her agreement. 'We're out of step with the majority, I think.'

'That's doesn't bother me one bit. But going to Hollywood with Mr Rayburn is another matter.'

'You must learn to call him Rick,' Katy said firmly, 'and you're definitely going to go. You've said yes, and I'm not letting you change your mind. I've a feeling in my bones it's going to be a great opportunity for you, Melissa.'

CHAPTER TWO

MELISSA had not travelled first class on a plane since childhood holidays with her parents, so it was something of a treat to find herself seated in a comfortable armchair beside Rick, drinking champagne and nibbling caviar, to the accompaniment of interested looks from their neighbours.

'I hope they're not bothering you too much,' her employer asked considerately, after several had stopped to speak to him and comment how much they'd enjoyed his last movie. 'It's a bit like sitting in a goldfish bowl, but at least I'm used to it.'

Unlike most celebrities of his standing, Rick did not travel with a retinue, but instead was usually accompanied by a girl-friend and a press officer. But on this occasion he had even dispensed with *his* services, as his American agent had arranged for one of their own men to take care of his publicity during his stay, and generally protect him from the prying eyes of the public.

'I don't think I'd like it on a permanent basis,' Melissa replied. 'But for a short while it's rather fun getting the celebrity treatment too!'

'Any girl travelling with me automatically becomes one,' Rick replied.

He was not wrong; Melissa had no doubt

there would be speculation in the tabloids about their relationship, and this would be picked up by the American papers as well—which suited Rick's purpose admirably. The seeds of doubt would be sown in his ex-wife's mind even before their arrival. The questions flung at them by the reporters at the airport had left her in no doubt of this. Too many famous people called their girl-friends secretaries for them to be believed, even when it happened to be true!

'And I must say you don't even look like one,' Rick went on. 'Those new clothes of yours have worked a small miracle.'

'On someone five feet two and a half, they couldn't work a large one!' Melissa quipped.

The actor chuckled. 'One thing I can say about you, Melissa, you never bore me. Even if we don't manage to fool Jessica, I won't regret taking you along.'

'Tell me something about our host,' Melissa said, preferring to keep the conversation on a less personal note. 'Do you know him well?'

'I don't think anyone could say they knew him well,' Rick answered drily. 'I met him several times during my marriage, but I always had the feeling he disapproved of me. He's an arrogant, supercilious son of a bitch. These upper-crust Yanks can be even worse snobs than our lot, and they don't come more upper-crust than Bartholomew Reed Huntingdon the Fourth.'

'The fourth?' Melissa smiled. 'How pretentious can you get? I thought only kings and queens had numbers after their names!'

'Well, he is heir apparent to one of the largest fortunes in the States. Mind you, I can't stand the guy personally, though he's not just a rich man's son. He has the reputation of being one of the brightest businessmen in the country, and speaks several languages fluently.'

'How old is this paragon?'

'Thirty-five or thereabouts.'

'Married?'

'Nope—and never has been. My guess is he can't find anyone good enough! Perfect pedigrees are hard to come by in this day and age, and from what Jessica's told me, he's dead set on preserving his own. These social register types guard their good names—though there are always a few black sheep who marry beneath them. Usually because that's where they were hooked!' Reflectively the actor sipped his champagne. 'But old Bartholomew is too cool a customer and too conscious of who he is to ever let his passions run away with him!'

'Yuck. I loathe him already.'

Rick smiled. 'Actually he can be quite a charmer when he wants, and as much as I hate to admit it, he's not bad-looking either.'

Coming from the actor that was quite a concession, and momentarily Melissa's interest was stirred. But then she remembered the other things she'd been told about him, and it quickly waned. The man sounded like a crass snob, a trait she positively despised.

Well, she doubted she'd have much in common with Bartholomew Reed Huntingdon the Fourth. Boy, what a mouthful! No wonder he wasn't married. What girl with any sense would want to be landed with that name?

After they'd eaten dinner, Rick joined two businessmen at the bar whom he'd met on a couple of previous flights, and Melissa didn't see him again until they were asked to fasten their safety belts in preparation for their landing at Los Angeles International Airport.

'What a shame it's dark,' she commented regretfully, as the plane headed towards the lights of the runway. 'It looks very pretty, but much like any other city at night.'

'Wait till you see it in the morning,' Rick enthused, 'particularly if it's a clear day. Beverly Hills in the sunlight is absolutely glorious.'

'Yet you prefer to live in London.'

'Living in heaven can become as unbearable as hell!' he replied. 'I prefer it in small doses. That way I can really appreciate it.'

By the time they were through with Customs—movie stars, like lesser mortals, were subjected to the same formalities—and more reporters and photographers, it was nearly ten o'clock. But at least there was no hanging around waiting in line for a cab. The smartly uniformed chauffeur who'd met them in the Arrivals Hall now whisked them outside into a black Rolls Camargue.

The first thing that struck Melissa was the intense heat, and she remarked on it.

'It takes some getting used to after England,' the chauffeur answered, 'but you'll find everywhere's air-conditioned, including the cars, so it really won't bother you too much.'

Within a few minutes he'd proved his point, and cool air enveloped them.

'Mr Huntingdon here yet?' Rick enquired.

'He arrived a few days ago,' the chauffeur answered. 'But he's in San Diego on business at the moment, and won't be back until after midnight.'

'How about Miss Welles?'

'She's at the house, Mr Rayburn, but she's entertaining guests tonight for dinner.'

'Probably to prove she doesn't give a damn about my arrival,' the actor growled *sotto voce* to Melissa. 'Typical!'

'She must have some redeeming qualities other than her sex-appeal, Mr Rayburn,' Melissa couldn't help saying. 'Otherwise you'd never have married her.

'If she did I've forgotten them. Divorce, American style, tends to have that effect. And for God's sake call me Rick!' he said under his breath.

The journey to the Huntingdon mansion, set on a hilltop over two thousand feet above Los Angeles, took well over an hour, and from what Melissa could make out in the dark, was totally secluded.

'If I ever go out on my own, I'll need radar to find my way back again,' she joked, as they drove through the bewildering maze of narrow, twisting roads that led there.

'It looks more complicated than it really is in the dark, Miss Abbot,' the chauffeur said reassuringly, and drew to a halt outside massive wrought-iron gates set into the high stone wall surrounding the property, and blasted his horn in some kind of code. Melissa assumed this because as soon as he had finished they swung open.

'It's easier to get in and out of Fort Knox than here,' Rick told her, 'and about the only security system they don't have is the National Guard!'

'With all the cranks around nowadays, we need everything we can get,' the chauffeur interjected. 'And at least you folks will be able to sleep soundly at night.'

For half a mile or so they wended their way along a floodlit, cypress-lined avenue, until they finally rounded a bend and saw the house before them. And what a house! Triple-storied, Moorish in style, with an arched and columned frontage, it was more like a gleaming white Sultan's palace.

'Cosy little place, isn't it?' Melissa murmured. 'We'll probably need a map to find the way to our bedrooms!'

Rick chuckled, 'Believe it or not, this place is hardly ever used. When the Huntingdons want to relax they go to one of their other hovels at Martha's Vineyard, Palm Beach, or Newport, Rhode Island.'

'What a waste to shut up anything as lovely as this for most of the year.'

'But it isn't,' the chauffeur informed her, as he removed their bags from the boot of the Rolls.' When the family aren't in residence, it's open to the public. There are so many beautiful things here, Mr Huntingdon decided it was only fair to allow them to be seen.'

'How old is the house?'

'It was built just before the turn of the century, and has forty rooms. It was bought by Mr Huntingdon's grandfather in 1932.

'You sound like a guide,' Melissa said, amused at the man's monotone recital.

'I am,' he answered surprisingly. 'That's my job when no one's living here, and the rest of the staff help out as well. The Huntingdons are good employers, Miss Abbot, and none of us minds doing whatever we're asked.'

As they passed through the massive arched,

nail-studded door, set in a smooth stone wall
between the east and west wings, they entered a
marble-clad hall that wouldn't have looked out
of place in a grand hotel. Tasteful *objets d'art*
caught the eye, and Melissa recognised Henry
Moore and at least two Rodins.

White-jacketed servants seemed to rush from
all sides, but it was not until they had disappeared
up the sweeping staircase with the luggage that
Melissa had her first real-life glimpse of Jessica
Welles.

The actress made her entrance—for that was
what it was—from one of the endless rooms
leading from the hall, and both in looks and
colouring was as exquisite as on the screen.

In her late thirties, like most fair people she
looked younger than her years. Tall, and reed-
slender, she had golden-blonde hair drawn
severely back into a chignon to expose a classical
oval face and features to match. She wore a long
silk dress in a Persian design of peacocks and
flowers, which almost exactly echoed the pattern
and colours of the rugs covering the floor, and
the side slit revealed slim, shapely legs.

Her slightly too small mouth was a flash of
glistening pink as it parted into a welcoming
smile to show small, pearly-white teeth, though
it did not reach her famous smoke-grey eyes as
she focused her full attention on Melissa, after
bestowing a welcoming kiss on her ex-husband's
cheek.

'Your pictures in the paper don't flatter you,'
she drawled, in her renowned husky voice, with
its almost imperceptible American accent. 'You're
not at all the downtrodden little secretary I'd
been expecting.'

'That's because I'm not in the least downtrodden,' Melissa answered sweetly. She had met too many well-known personages to be overawed, even by this one, and her Yves St Laurent suit gave an extra boost to her confidence. 'Rick . . . I mean Mr Rayburn,' deliberately she made the error, 'is a most considerate employer.'

'That's more than I can say of him as a husband!' the actress's eyes glinted.

'We've plenty of time to start throwing insults at each other tomorrow,' the man under discussion interposed. 'Do you think I could have a drink? My throat's parched. It's all that damned air-conditioning in the car.'

'But of course, darling.' Jessica was all concern. 'How about you,?' she flung at Melissa. 'Would you care to join us, or would you rather go straight to your room?' It was obvious from her tone which she preferred.

'I think I'd rather go straight to my room,' Melissa answered. 'I am rather tired.'

'One of the servants will show you the way.' The actress pressed a bell set in the wall. 'Are you strictly a shorthand and typing secretary, or do you have other talents?' she enquired matter-of-factly. 'Depending on your answer, I'll know what room to put you in.'

'We don't sleep together, if that's what you really want to know, Jessica,' the actor interjected.

'Now or never?'

Melissa geared herself for battle. Obviously the actress was determined to be bitchy rather than friendly. But forewarned was forearmed, and if that was the way she wanted to play it, she'd show her she'd met her match.

'I'm afraid if you want to know the answer to that you'll have to bug the bedrooms—or have you already done it?' Melissa cooed.

Behind his ex-wife's back, Rick winked at Melissa and mouthed *'Touché'*.

The entrance of a manservant precluded further discussion on that particular topic, and after Jessica had instructed him to take Melissa to the blue room in the west wing, she linked arms with Rick. Then with a cool goodnight to Melissa, she turned on her four-inch heels, and led him into the room she had recently vacated.

Melissa followed the servant to the next floor and then along an infinite corridor to the west wing. Here she found an enchanting suite furnished in shades of blue and white silk, with a draped and pleated four-poster bed, and Moroccan carved doors on all the fitted cupboards.

The en suite bathroom had a sunken white marble tub, large enough in which to swim several strokes, and the walls of the small sitting-room were, like the bed, draped and pleated in powder blue and white silk. All that was needed to complete the picture of an Arabian Nights dream were the dancing girls, and a sheikh!

Melissa was too exhausted to do full justice to the plate of smoked salmon sandwiches sent up to her, but drank several cups of the excellent coffee.

Although it was only three o'clock in the afternoon time-wise, as far as she was concerned, her travel-weary body proclaimed otherwise, and she decided to have a bath, take a sleeping pill—something she rarely did, but it would help

her adjust more quickly to the time difference—
and go to bed.

It came as almost no surprise to find that the
water that flowed from the gold-plated taps was
tinted exactly the same shade of blue as the
carpet, nor that it was scented as well! Like the
pile of bestsellers on the bookshelf in the
bedroom—hardback of course—and the remote-
control colour television set, it was one more
indication of how the super-rich lived. Well, for
a few weeks she'd wallow in the sheer luxury of
it all, and see if at the end she agreed with her
employer's assertion that too much of a good
thing could become boring.

Her sleep was dreamless, and she awoke at
seven completely refreshed. The sun streamed
through the windows, and smogless blue sky
could be glimpsed, so that as she stepped out on
to her balcony to look at the view of Los
Angeles and the surrounding hills of Bel Air,
there was no haze to spoil its magnificence.

Below her, in the flower-filled garden with its
tinkling fountains, a fierce-looking Great Dane
was being put through its paces by a tracksuited
man, who then rewarded the dog's obedience
with a game of ball. Obviously the animal's
handler, Melissa thought, for, in spite of its
great size, the dog was as gentle as a lamb with
him.

After a glass of fresh orange juice from the
silver thermos by her bed, Melissa decided to
have a swim before breakfast. Donning a brief
bikini, and a matching citrus-yellow cover-all,
she slipped out of her room and down the
staircase.

The house was strangely quiet, but she had no

doubt the staff were up and about, and some time later, when she'd completely lost her bearings in the vast grounds, she wished one of them would appear and direct her to the pool. Thankfully, when she found herself beside the tennis courts, she saw the tracksuited man who'd been playing with the dog.

He was about to unlatch the wire gate leading into the courts, but when she touched him on the shoulder, he swung round with a start.

'What are you doing up at this hour?' he enquired roughly.

'I wasn't aware there were any rules and regulations about it,' she answered coolly, taken aback at his brusqueness.

'There aren't—but I don't like people creeping up on me.'

'It's hard to make any noise walking on grass, unless you have bells attached to your feet!' she retorted. 'Next time, I'll remember to wear them.'

For a moment he looked as if he might smile. But he resisted the temptation. Obviously a man who took himself very seriously. He was about thirty-five, Melissa surmised, for, in spite of the grey hair which swept back from his forehead like a veritable lion's mane, the face beneath was almost unlined.

He was undeniably attractive too: slanting light brown eyes, that could at calmer times be the colour of sherry, but which were now, with thunder signs in them, a deeper incandescent colour, a long straight nose down which he was staring at her superciliously, and an extremely determined jawline, redeemed from harshness by an unexpected dimple in the chin. His mouth was thin but well-shaped, and as uncompromisingly hard as the rest of his features. Not surprisingly in this glorious climate, he was tanned a rich golden brown, and she thought whimsically, how well his strong-looking face would have fitted on to the prow of a Viking ship.

'You must be Melissa Abbot,' he said.

She nodded. Obviously all the staff in this smoothly run household were primed with the names of guests, whatever their job.

'I saw you playing with your dog from my balcony. He's a marvellous-looking animal.'

'*She,*' the man corrected. 'And don't let our little game of ball fool you into believing she's a pet. If you ever see her loose in the grounds— or any other dogs for that matter, I advise you to stand still. If you run, they'll go straight for the jugular.'

'Has anyone ever told you you have a wonderful knack of making people feel at home?' she enquired sweetly.

'Better frightened than mauled,' he answered flatly.

Melissa fingered her throat gingerly. 'If they're that vicious, I hope Mr Huntingdon's well insured. I'm rather fond of my neck the way it is.'

There was a silence while he studied it, and she wondered if he'd thought she was fishing for a compliment. But if he had, one wasn't forthcoming.

'Do you think you could direct me to the pool?' she asked after a few moments. 'Your conversation is absolutely scintillating, but I really must tear myself away!'

This time he managed a slight smile—thought it was not an apologetic one, in spite of her obvious rebuke—and she had a glimpse of strong, even white teeth.

'I'll do better than that,' he answered. 'I'll take you there myself. Until you're used to the grounds, finding your way round can be something of a problem.'

His voice was as attractive as his appearance: firm yet quick and unexpectedly deep and, like Jessica Welle's accent, his was clipped, so that he sounded almost English. Well educated, too, and Melissa wondered if he was a victim of the recession. Certainly he seemed the type of man more used to giving orders than taking them, and perhaps this accounted for the chip he appeared to have on his shoulder.

Close to six feet, the guard had a gait that was well co-ordinated and upright, giving the impression of athleticism and, if his pace was anything to go by, his speciality was the hundred-yard dash! He made no concession for Melissa's far smaller strides, and she had to almost run to keep up with him, so that she barely had time to admire the luxuriously planted vases and tubs of many-coloured flowers, the rose bushes and azaleas set in borders of clipped box amid neatly gravelled paths, or the octagonal summer house with an ogival roof, which reminded her of a picture she'd once seen in a magazine of something similiar at Mount Vernon, in which George Washington gave his step-grandchildren their lessons.

'It's an exact replica,' the grey-haired man told her, when she commented on it.

'All this must take some looking after,' she

remarked, as they passed through an ornamental gate.

'Five gardeners work here full time,' he supplied briefly.

'If it takes this long to reach the pool, I'll have to get up even earlier in future,' she said.

'There's a far quicker way from the house,' he answered. 'But I thought you might enjoy a small tour.'

'Do *you* act as a guide as well?' Melissa enquired.

'As well as what?' he asked, slowing his pace.

'As well as your other duties,' she said.

'Only with family guests, not the general public,' he replied.

Melissa would like to have questioned him about the family, but he didn't strike her as the type who would be very forthcoming. In fact he'd probably resent it. He was the tight-lipped loyal sort, not a back-stair gossip.

The pool, when she saw it, appeared even larger than it had looked from her bedroom balcony, and would not have been out of place in a hotel accommodating a couple of hundred guests. Circular in shape, and terazza-tiled in an intricate design of green and gold, it had several sunken seating areas nearby, as well as luxurious lounging chairs, hammocks and umbrellas.

'The jacuzzi and changing rooms are through there,' the man said, pointing to a pergola.

'Be it ever so humble, there's no place like home!' Melissa murmured, though more with admiration than sarcasm, for only a puritan would not be impressed with the sheer beauty of the design and setting. 'It's the most exquisite pool I've ever seen,' she added for her companion's benefit, in case he thought her comment had been a criticism of his employer's wealth.

But it was impossible to judge what was in his mind, for his expression as he turned to face her was neutral.

'The house is through there,' he said, indicating a path through a sub-tropical garden. 'It's only twenty yards away, and if you haven't already eaten, breakfast is served from eight o'clock until ten. Enjoy your swim,' he added, before walking away in the direction from which they had come.

After fifteen minutes' leisurely crawl in the cool water, Melissa's stomach gave her a rebellious reminder that she'd not eaten for more than sixteen hours; she followed the security guard's directions, and within minutes found herself beneath an arched patio, where Jessica Welles and Rick were already seated at a glass-topped table. They were in the process of an argument, which stopped abruptly when Melissa said, 'Good morning.'

'Melissa, sweetheart,' Rick greeted her with a relieved smile. 'Why didn't you wake me? I'd have had a swim with you.'

'You know you hate being disturbed,' she trilled, while at the same time wondering where the heck his bedroom *was*.

'Not by you,' he leered.

Jessica, dressed in a housecoat of softest pink, silky corn-gold hair tumbling loosely around her perfectly featured face, looked ethereal, and Melissa marvelled at the change from the feline creature of last night. But the woman was a first-rate actress, and was able to use her chameleon-like talent adroitly to take up whatever persona was appropriate to her mood. And this morning it was sweet innocence.

'Richard has been singing your praises, Melissa,' she said, 'It seems you're responsible for seeing my alimony cheque always arrives on time!'

'I wouldn't want you to go hungry, Miss Welles,' Melissa smiled, seating herself beside her employer.

'Watch out for her, Melissa,' Rick warned. 'When Jessica refers to me as Richard, you can bet she's on the warpath!'

'From what I've heard so far, your little secretary's well able to take care of herself.' The actress looked across at Melissa, eyes hard as pebbles, although a smile hovered on the small, full-lipped mouth.

'Not if this morning's any indication,' a man's voice said from behind. It was instantly recognisable as the security guard's, and a moment later he was bending over to kiss the actress on the cheek. 'Your elephant,' he smiled, dropping what looked like a jewelled gold charm on to her empty plate. 'Just where you said it would be, on the centre court.' He turned his attention to Rick, holding out his hand by way of a greeting. 'Nice to see you again. I hope your room's comfortable, and everything else is satisfactory?'

'It has to be, doesn't it?' Rick answered, not attempting to hide his feelings. 'I gather you've already met my right arm,' he went on. 'How come?'

'She couldn't find the pool.' Sherry-brown eyes focused on Melissa. 'Enjoy your swim?'

Mortified, she could only stare back at him. So this was her host! No wonder he'd acted as if he owned the place—and what an idiot she now felt for not recognising that he did! Irritated at being mistaken for a member of his staff, he'd played along, knowing the embarrassment it would cause her when she discovered the truth. It was a lousy thing to do, and added to the dislike she'd felt for him.

'Very much, thank you,' she finally managed to say, making sure her tone lacked any warmth.

'How's your family?' Rick asked politely, and Melissa knew him well enough to be aware that he wasn't in the least bit interested.

'Fine,' came the brief reply, indicating that the other man was aware of it too.

There was an uneasy silence, and Melissa wondered if this was a portent of things to come. If so, it was going to be a tedious few weeks.

'Ted Edson will be over this afternoon to discuss the shooting schedule,' Bartholomew Huntingdon named the director of the movie. 'Or has Jessica already told you that?'

Rick nodded. 'I'd have preferred to wait until tomorrow. I find it difficult to concentrate on anything serious when I'm suffering from jet-lag.'

'You didn't exactly go to bed late,' his ex-wife interjected. 'Or perhaps you didn't go to sleep straight away,' she added with a meaningful glance at Melissa, who was concentrating on her croissant as if her life depended on it.

A silver pot of coffee was placed on the table by a white-coated houseman, and once again silence reigned while he filled all their cups.

'Why not take a look at the breakfast menu,

Melissa?' Rick passed it to her. 'Your appetite's too healthy to be satisfied with a couple of small croissants.'

The implication was that she breakfasted with him regularly, and conscious of the stare of her host, she was suddenly embarrassed by the charade. But only momentarily. Then her good sense returned. Bartholomew Reed Huntingdon the Fourth was nothing to her, and if she *was* having an affair with her boss, it was no business of his.

'You're always so considerate,' she breathed, throwing Rick an affectionate glance before concentrating on the menu.

Everything imaginable was on it, from cereal to kedgeree. But they were too English and she plumped for waffles, bacon, maple syrup and butter.

'I suppose you dieted before you came away,' the actress enquired. 'That's what I usually do.'

'You've no need to diet any more than Melissa has,' her ex-husband said.

'The camera puts on pounds,' she replied, 'and *you'd* do well to remember it. The last movie we made together they had to let your clothes out a couple of inches half-way through.'

'We were on location in the South of France,' he explained to Melissa. 'And those three-star restaurants broke even *my* iron will.'

'Bart's chef used to work in one—that's why I'm warning you,' Jessica said. 'You're playing the hero, darling, and whoever heard of one with a paunch!'

Rick chuckled good-humouredly. 'You'll have to tell your chef to keep the food simple—for me, at least,' he requested their host.

'Where did he work, Mr Huntingdon?' Melissa
enquired curiously.

'At Papa Hardi's,' he answered. 'And please
call me Bart.'

'I'm glad you abbreviate your name.' Melissa
couldn't stop herself saying what she was
thinking.

'She's not too smitten with Reed Huntingdon
the Fourth,' Rick interjected mischievously. 'I'm
inclined to agree with her that it's a bit
pretentious.'

The glint in their host's eyes signified his
awareness of being baited. 'Is it the Reed
Huntingdon she objects to, or the Fourth?' he
asked urbanely.

Melissa knew she was being put down, and
was annoyed with Rick for provoking it.

'Bartholomew's a family name, and so is
Reed, and all firstborn sons are saddled with
it,' he went to explain. 'I'm the firstborn son of
the fourth generation—hence the number!'

'Bart's ancestors came over on the *Mayflower*
with mine.' Jessica came into the conversation
again. 'So we've been connected since time
immemorial.'

Rick grinned wickedly. 'Time immemorial to
you Yanks isn't even history to us, darling!'

But if the intention had been to rile her,
Jessica refused to accept the challenge, and let
the comment go with a gracious smile.

Melissa's waffles arrived, and she attacked
them with gusto.

'You're going to get mighty sick of them,'
her host said.

'As long as your chef doesn't get tired of

making them, I'll never tire of eating them,'
she vowed.

'He'll make whatever you want—that's his
job,' came the sober reply. 'If there's anything
he can't stand, it's having his cooking rejected.'

'I can understand that. Whatever job you
have, you like to know it's appreciated.'

'Still in the wine business?' Rick enquired.

Bart looked surprised at the question.
'We don't normally close down a profitable
company,' he answered.

'I only asked because I haven't noticed your
label lately at my wine merchant's, and when I
mentioned it to them, they told me they could
no longer get it.'

'Give me their name, and I'll find out why.'
Bart produced a small crocodile notebook from
the pocket of his tracksuit. 'This year's vintage
is one of our best,' he said as he wrote. 'I'll
serve it with lunch. Perhaps you'll let me have
your opinion of it.'

'Now I know why *Newsweek* and *Forbes*
magazine refer to you as a human computer,'
Rick flattered. 'With all your vast interests, to
be bothered by one small complaint, and
actually *do* something about it, is really
something.'

'From little seeds big apples grow,' Bart
Huntingdon shrugged off the compliment.

'Are your vineyards anywhere near here, Mr
Hunt—Bart?' Melissa asked.

'Near in American terms, but not English,'
he answered. 'Napa is about three hundred
and fifty miles away.'

'Do you give conducted tours? I know some
of the vineyards do.'

He nodded. 'Interested?'

'I would be, if it wasn't so far,' she smiled.

'I'll arrange for you to be flown down there. All you need do is name the day.'

'It sounds a good idea.' Rick squeezed Melissa's hand as she smiled her thanks for the offer. 'I don't want you getting bored hanging around the set every day watching me.'

Unaware that this had been his intention, Melissa made no comment.

'Have you been to California before?' It was Bart Huntingdon again.

'No.' Rick spoke for her. 'I've promised to give her a tour of all the local sights myself though. I want my little Melissa to play rather than work while she's here. She's a marvellous secretary, and deserves a bit of spoiling.'

'I hope you won't mind if she does *some* work,' the actress said. 'I was going to ask if I could borrow her to do some letters for me this morning.'

'With pleasure,' he answered smoothly. 'But what's happened to your own? You used to keep three on the go.'

'I still do—but I left them back in New York as Bart always provides someone. Unfortunately all the girls at his office are tied up today, aren't they, darling?'

'That's right, so we'll use Melissa to take notes of our talk with Ted Edson as well,' he said.

'Sure,' Rick agreed. 'I'd have wanted her with me anyway.'

'Perhaps you'll come up to my room in about an hour?' Jessica addressed Melissa as she rose. 'I'll be dressed by then.'

'Are you in the west wing as well?'

'No—that's only for guests. I come under the category of family. But Richard will direct you. He knows how to get there.'

Their host departed with her, leaving Melissa alone with Rick.

'You've stayed here before then?' she asked.

'Once—when we were married. Why?' he grinned. 'Did you think I'd been to her room last night.'

'Hardly, as she thought you'd been to mine!' Melissa replied drily. 'But even if you had, Mr Rayburn, it's not my business to object—except that it seems pointless my being here if you're going to give in to your instincts without a fight.'

'I've heard sex called some tactful names in my time,' he chuckled, 'but none as quaint as that! In spite of your general broad-mindedness, Melissa, there's something essentially old-fashioned about you.' He toyed idly with a spoon, twirling it between his fingers. 'But to get back to Jessica. I've no intention of sleeping with her. Seeing her again, and being reminded of what a bitch she is, has made me even more determined. In fact, I was rather annoyed with you last night when you went up to bed and left me alone with her.'

'I'm sorry about that—but I thought you'd wanted to be, and that's why you'd asked for a drink.' Melissa dabbed at her mouth with the pink linen napkin. 'Do you think she really needs me for those letters, or is it an excuse to question me about you?'

'It doesn't make much odds either way. I

think we've already made it pretty obvious our relationship is more than a working one.'

'Where's *your* room, by the way?' Melissa asked.

'Right next to yours—where else?'

'By special request, no doubt?'

'How clever of you to guess.' He stretched lazily. 'I think I'll take the script and spend the morning by the pool going over it. There's no point in learning my lines until I know the shooting schedule from Ted.'

One of the most disconcerting things Melissa had discovered about filming, was that it did not necessarily follow the given story line, and scenes were often shot completely out of context.

'I suppose you'll want me to hear them when you do?' she said.

Although he could remember lines almost on sight, Rick liked to use her as a sounding board before actually speaking them on the set

'At least you can get yourself a tan at the same time,' he smiled. 'But take care you don't burn. I don't want my beautiful English peach turning into a dried Californian prune!'

After directing her to Jessica's room, he left her at the door of her own.

'Got everything you want in there?' he questioned.

'And more besides,' she smiled. 'I found a selection of perfume in one of my bathroom cupboards this morning. There must be every make imaginable, and all unopened. What I'd like to know is, what do they do with the started ones?'

'You're expected to take them with you when

you leave,' he told her. 'I remember Bart once telling me one of his guests took the whole lot—and she was almost as rich as he is!'

'Everybody likes something for nothing, no matter how much money they have,' Melissa commented. 'But don't worry, Mr Rayburn. I'll choose *one*, and use it the whole time I'm here.'

'For goodness' sake stop calling me Mr Rayburn,' he said irritably.

'I know I have to call you Rick in public, but I wasn't sure what you wanted me to do in private.'

'It would look damned funny if someone overheard you. We're supposed to be twentieth-century lovers, honey, not characters out of *Pride and Prejudice*!'

Changing into a cotton blouse and a matching floral-sprigged skirt, Melissa speculated on the relationship between Bart Huntingdon and Jessica Welles. Had they been lovers at any time? Or were they now? They'd certainly not given any indication if they were, but then neither of them were the type to show their emotions: the woman because she was too good an actress, the man because he was extremely self-contained.

It was difficult to decide whether she liked him or not. Her first impression had certainly not been favourable. But he *had* offered to fly her down to see his vineyard, and though it probably didn't put him out much, as he'd made it plain he'd no intention of accompanying her—and why should he?—it had still been a nice gesture. Well, time would tell. This was a charade she'd entered into with some trepidation, but at least all the cast were now assembled and their roles fairly well defined. It was now a question of making sure her own performance was good enough to be convincing. Rick, with his usual professionalism, had already slipped into *his* part with consummate ease.

CHAPTER THREE

Looking back on her first four weeks in Los Angeles, Melissa was surprised at how quickly they had flown. After the first day, Jessica had not asked her to do any more letters for her, though she'd been generous in her praise for Melissa's speed and efficiency. Her request had turned out to be genuine enough: business correspondence in the main, and a couple of letters to friends abroad.

Cleverly, she'd not attempted to question Melissa directly about her relationship with Rick, remarking instead on the suit she had worn the previous evening when she'd arrived, and enquiring where she'd bought it, how much it had cost, and if she often shopped at Rive Gauche. But even though it was obvious Melissa could not afford to go there on a secretary's wage, however generous, she made no comment, nor did she do so when Melissa continued to appear in outfits not commensurate with her position. With Rick's innuendos there was little need.

An arm lingering affectionately around her shoulders just a little longer than was necessary, a more than friendly pat on the bottom, and eyes continually resting on her—a picture was gradually emerging of a man trying to keep his obsession for a much younger girl in check. It was a subtle and clever performance, and one that Melissa was beginning to admire more than any of his screen ones.

'We played our first love scene today, and though Jessica tried every trick she knew, I managed not to respond,' Rick reported back to Melissa jubilantly. 'I just closed my eyes and thought of half a million dollars a year more in my bank account!'

Of their host they saw little. Every day, as soon as Rick and Jessica had been dispatched in the studio car, Bart was driven to his Los Angeles headquarters. There was a helicopter pad on the estate too, and sometimes he made use of that, speeding off to some outlying area to inspect factories manufacturing items as diversified as computers and canned fruit.

The Huntingdon Corporation's interests were worldwide, though, and during the year Bart made a point of visiting as many as possible. Melissa had been curious to discover if there were any particular ones that engaged his interest more than the rest.

'Not really,' he had answered, when she'd broached the question one evening over dinner. 'All business is a challenge, and when you head a sizeable company, one part of it is very much like another. It's the mechanics that fascinate me, which is why I'm often labelled obsessive by the press.' He'd given a rueful smile. 'I guess it's justified, as, other than tennis and my morning jog, I have few outside interests.'

'What about your porcelain collection?' Melissa questioned. 'I seem to remember Rick mentioning you'd even written a book on it that other experts regard as definitive.'

'That's true,' he acknowledged, a man with no time for false modesty. 'Seventeenth and eighteenth-century Sèvres and Limoges are my speciality. But even that's something of a business with me. However much I admire a piece when I buy it, I can't resist a profit if I'm offered one.' He'd shrugged. 'Crazy, isn't it? I don't need to tell you it has nothing to do with the actual money. I guess wheeling and dealing is in my blood.'

There was no reason not to believe him about the money part. He had more than he could spend in several lifetimes, and, like the rest of his family, was admired for the amounts he gave away.

Not that Bart himself had mentioned this to her, nor had she learned it from Rick. For some reason Melissa had wanted to keep her curiosity a secret. Instead, with time on her hands, she'd taken herself to the library of a newspaper and looked up their back files.

Gossip about his private life had been of particular interest. He had escorted a succession of well-known beauties, the type of girls whose only claim to fame was as companions of the super-rich, and who flitted from one to the other. His name often appeared in the society columns as well, but his companions here were generally of the more stolid variety. But then, Melissa decided, it would be an unfair world if every millionaire's daughter was beautiful as well! None of Bart's affairs seemed to last long, though, and there had never been any hint of

marriage, although there was plenty of speculation about it.

Towards Melissa, he behaved with complete
detachment, giving the impression he had better
things to do than bother with her. Not that he
was rude, just distant, displaying the same cool
politeness at the end of the fourth week, as he
had at the beginning of her first.

Because of this withdrawal, both in the physical
and mental sense, most evenings when there
were no guests he disappeared immediately after
dinner, and Melissa was left with Rick as her
sole companion. By this time too, Jessica
appeared to have become resigned to her ex-
husband's infatuation, and other than when Bart
entertained and she acted as his hostess, the
actress rarely even ate with them, spending her
time instead with other friends.

Although it was a situation Melissa had
anticipated to some extent, she had not anticipated the mind-bending boredom. The actor's
conversation centred upon himself, and any
attempt to divert him resulted in a sulky silence.
Basically the movie business was all that
interested him, and he was at a loss discussing
most things outside it, rarely picking up a
newspaper, and confining his reading matter to
scripts sent to him by his agent.

To be the centre of attention, to hold court,
have people fawn over him, was his life-blood,
and though he could be kind, and even
considerate on occasions, she was beginning to
realise that even this was to feed his ego. How
true the adage that you never knew someone
until you lived wih them for twenty-four hours a
day!

Yet surely the compensations outweighed the drawbacks? Melissa asked herself one evening as she was changing for dinner. True to his word, Rick had given her a grand tour of the sights of Los Angeles. She had also accompanied him to several parties thrown by famous screen personalities, where each attempted to outdo the other in originality and extravagance, not only in the style and décor of their homes, but in the food they served. It was a world she had glimpsed in London, and one that continued to intrigue her, though she viewed it very much as an outsider who was aware she could never feel part of it. It was too insular, as well as too flamboyant.

If Bart Huntingdon had similar thoughts, he did not openly express them, although it was implicit in his refusal to attend these junkets, and the fact that he rarely reciprocated the invitations. When he himself entertained, he was an excellent host, and there was always a relaxed atmosphere to the gatherings, in spite of the grandeur of the surroundings.

Melissa reflected about his other residences scattered over the globe. It seemed Huntingdons rarely deigned to stay anywhere as mundane as a hotel, and most of their office blocks contained an apartment for the family's private use. When they did not, there were always friends with villas.

It was a privileged existence, and one completely sheltered from reality. Was Bart aware of the world outside? Melissa wondered, as she paused for one final critical look at herself in the mirror, before going downstairs. It was a question she would never ask him, for she would have to be on far more intimate terms to attempt it. And as they had not spent more than five minutes alone with each other since their first meeting, this was unlikely.

Was it conceit that made her piqued by his lack of interest? She frowned. What else could it be?

'Melissa?' Rick, knocking at her door, interrupted her flow of thought.

'Yes?' she questioned as she opened it.

'I thought we might as well go down together if you were ready,' he smiled. 'And I can see you are. You look lovely. That chiffon is almost the same shade as your eyes.'

'I'm glad you like it,' she answered demurely.

'Which reminds me,' he said, as she picked up a matching soft leather pochette. 'Have you got an appropriate dress for Vegas? We're invited to a Tom Jones gala, and everyone who's anyone will be there. All the women will be dressed to kill, and I'd like *you* to knock them all dead!'

Location scenes for the movie were being shot at Caesar's Palace, and the whole crew were moving in there for a week. Naturally Melissa was accompanying Rick.

'I'm flattered you think I could,' she smiled, though under no illusions herself. 'But I think you've seen the whole of my wardrobe during the past few weeks. Isn't there anything that will do?'

His wide mouth lifted whimsically at the corners. 'Not really. I'd like you to wear something far more eyecatching—beaded and shimmering. You know the kind of thing?'

Indeed Melissa did. It was the Hollywood uniform. 'I'll look like a fairy on a Christmas tree,' she warned. 'With my height, I look better in plain things.'

But he wouldn't hear of it. 'Go to Neiman Marcus tomorrow,' he instructed. 'I've an account there, and I'll call them and tell them you're coming in.'

The prospect of wasting several thousand dollars on a dress she would never put on her back again appalled Melissa, even though it was not her money she was being asked to spend. The only consolation was that if Rick wasn't wasting it on her, he'd be wasting it on someone else, and at least she might be able to sell it afterwards, and send the proceeds to charity.

As they walked down the curving staircase, with its delicate wrought-iron balustrade, Melissa caught a glimpse of herself in one of the gilded mirrors between the ormolu wall-brackets. Her low neckline showed off the tan she had acquired since she'd been here, and this in turn had brightened her red-gold hair, and made her eyes look a lighter, smoky aquamarine. Her eyelashes were unusually dark, and she rarely did anything to increase their length. But tonight she'd put on several coats of black mascara, enjoying the way they grew thicker and longer. She had no intention of batting them at Rick, though. The last thing *he* needed was encouragement!

After drinks in the main salon, dinner was served in the 'small' dining-room, the table glittering with Baccarat crystal. The guests were formally attired, the men suave in white dinner jackets, the women exquisitely jewelled and begowned. As usual the food was French, as were the dishes it was served on: blue, and gold Limoges. The cutlery was gold too, and the tablecloth pure silk damask, embroidered with real gold thread. There were also gold candelabra as centrepieces, with flowers cascading from their delicate brackets, their candles casting a soft glow.

'You're very quiet, little lady.' This from the Texan oil-man on Melissa's right. 'I guess you must find our politics pretty boring.'

'Quite the contrary,' she assured him hastily. 'But I do find them strange—your system's so different from our own.'

'Don't worry, I find them strange too!' This, surprisingly, from Bart at the head of the table, where she had thought him to be engrossed with the pretty brunette at his side. 'I'm a great admirer of the English system, and wish ours was more like it. Money and influence count for far too much here, and ability comes a poor third.'

Melissa agreed, but had not wished to voice her opinion for fear of offending. Nothing was more calculated to put people's backs up than criticisms of one's host country while enjoying its hospitality.

Bart's comment began a heated discussion that lasted throughout most of the meal, with Melissa contributing her fair share, and displaying— contrary to the impression she had given—a good working knowledge of American politics.

'You've obviously lived in the States,' her neighbour commented admiringly.

Melissa shook her head. 'This is only my second visit,' she said. 'But as our closest ally and the country that exerts the most influence on us, I'm naturally interested in everything that goes on here.'

'The same can't be said in reverse,' Rick interjected. 'Poor old England's lucky if she warrants a paragraph a week, unless one of our Royals happens to be holidaying with a pretty girl-friend!'

There was general laughter, and Rick went on to regale the party with stories of his many meetings with the Royal Family, one of whom he'd taken out to dinner a few times, and even been invited by her to her holiday home.

He was an excellent raconteur and, with all eyes upon him, he was in his element. Although Melissa had heard all of his stories before, she listened with interest just the same, as he always managed to bring a freshness to them.

When the meal finally ended, and the twenty-four-strong party returned to the main drawing-room, Rick immediately came over to her, while Bart mingled among his guests, Jessica at his side.

'How about a stroll on the terrace?' he suggested. 'With this blasted air-conditioning, it's warmer outside than in.'

'Good idea,' she agreed, suppressing a yawn.

It was nearly half-past twelve, but no one had made a move to leave and until they did, there was no way she could, without appearing rude. Sitting in the sunshine doing nothing was more tiring than working, and with the set closed to all outsiders—on Jessica's insistence—for a particularly passionate love scene between the actress and Rick, this was how Melissa had passed the last few days.

Hand in hand they wandered outside, though as soon as they were away from view, Melissa disengaged herself.

'There's no need to shy away from me as soon as we're alone,' Rick said in an aggrieved tone. 'I haven't got leprosy, you know!'

'Just warm hands,' Melissa teased.

'It's better than a cold heart.' He was still peeved. 'You make it obvious I don't exactly set you alight.'

'That's because I've been the confidante of too many of your old flames!' she quipped. 'Who was it said no man is a mystery to his secretary?'

'Probably you,' he replied gloomily. 'It sounds like the sort of thing you *would* say.'

Melissa smiled. 'If cold showers have stopped working, I'm quite willing to give you permission to cheat on me!'

'But it's you I damn well fancy cheating *with*!' he growled. 'I don't understand why it's taken me so long to realise how attractive you are, Melissa.'

'It's only the sultry evenings and the Californian moonlight that makes you think it now!' Melissa assured him, attempting tact rather than a direct rebuttal. 'And you wouldn't like to spoil a perfect working relationship when we're transported back into the cold light of a rainy English day, would you?'

'Who says it would be spoiled? Making love to you wouldn't change anything.'

'I think it would. And I like you too much to risk it.'

'For God's sake stop treating me like some pimply adolescent,' he said irritably. 'I'm not used to being patronised.'

'Would you rather I pretended feelings I don't possess?'

'You wouldn't be the first woman to do *that*,'

he answered sourly. 'And anyway, I'm not
convinced you don't fancy me. Why not relax a
little and give yourself a chance to see?'

Melissa decided the only thing to do was tell
him the truth—though whether he believed it
was another matter.

'Because I'm still a virgin,' she confessed in a
rush, observing his surprise with secret amusement. 'And when I do finally sleep with someone,
it'll be the man I intend to marry.' She paused.
'I assume your proposal didn't include a wedding
ring, Rick?'

'You know damn well it didn't.' He pulled her
close to him, and stared down into her eyes.
'You wouldn't be lying to me, would you?'

'Now why would I do that?' she asked
indignantly. 'Any girl would give her eye-teeth
to be propositioned by *you*, and if I hadn't made
a vow of chastity when I was confirmed, I
wouldn't hesitate.'

Her reply seemed to satisfy him. Perhaps he'd
rather believe her story than face the fact that
she might not fancy him.

'My luck Mary Poppins is the real you!' he
sighed resignedly.

'Now you know it, perhaps you'll let me off
that shopping expedition to Neiman Marcus?'
she suggested hopefully.

'Absolutely not. I want you to outdazzle
everybody,' he reiterated, 'and you're striking
enough to do it. You'll probably be the only
redhead there whose colour doesn't come out of
a bottle!'

The following morning when Melissa arrived
at the store, and entered the model dress

department as instructed, she was greeted by name.

'Miss Melissa Abbot?' the assistant enquired.

'Yes, but how on earth——?'

'Mr Rayburn gave us a description of you when he phoned to tell us you'd be coming in, and you're really quite unmistakable.'

It appeared Rick had not trusted her taste, and had given specific instructions regarding the type of dresses she was to be shown. She finally decided on a Geoffrey Beene. Short, and completely beaded, the skirt was in shaded waves of matt and shiny silver, the long-sleeved, loose three-quarter top, high-necked at the front and plunging nearly to her waist at the back, in black sequins.

But when the saleswoman told her the price, she gasped out loud and instantly rejected it.

'All the other designer-labelled models I've shown you are more or less the same,' the woman informed her. 'But you've no need to worry, Miss Abbot, it's still way below Mr Rayburn's limit.'

'I don't care what his credit rating is, I——' Melissa cut herself short as the blue-rinsed head shook, indicating that she'd misunderstood.

'It has nothing to do with his credit rating at the store,' she was assured politely. 'That's limitless anyway. I meant the amount he intended you to spend.'

Melissa shrugged slender shoulders resignedly, and asked for the dress to be packed.

While this was being done, she headed for the shoe department, purchasing a pair of silk, strappy evening pumps to go with the dress, and a pair of comfortable flatties in pastel pink that

went with the outfit she was wearing, and a
couple of others in her wardrobe. Afterwards
she made her way to the fur department, where,
the saleslady had informed her, there was a
special offer on white mink.

'Marvellous over your dress,' she'd enthused,
no doubt assuming that Melissa's hesitation over
the prize of the Geoffrey Beene had been little
more than an act for her benefit.

But Melissa's intention was not to spend any
more of her employer's money, but her own.
She'd spied a sporty-looking black mink and
leather coat in the window, which was also
reduced. It was not cheap, but then in a store of
this class one would not expect it to be. But
compared to anything of similar quality she'd
seen in London, it was a real snap, even taking
into account the duty she would have to pay
when she declared it.

Unlike other coats she'd tried on, this didn't
overpower her, and she decided to buy it. It was
the most expensive item of clothing she'd ever
owned, but there was nothing showy about it,
and she could wear it at home without causing
any comment from her friends, other than
admiration and perhaps envy at the price!

Annoyingly, when she went to pay for it she
discovered she'd left not only her traveller's
cheques behind, but her credit cards as well, and
she only had a hundred dollars in cash on her. It
must have happened when she'd changed hand-
bags in a rush this morning, when the taxi she'd
ordered had arrived much sooner than she'd
anticipated.

Melissa explained her predicament, and asked
if the coat could be put by for her. Unfortunately,

because it was on sale, the assistant apologetically refused.

'I'll be back this afternoon,' Melissa assured the manager, who had been called over for consultation.

'It might be here, it might not,' he said. 'I'm afraid it's such a bargain I can't give any guarantee, and we've already had it out of the window twice this morning before you.'

It was then Melissa remembered Rick's account with the store. Of course. She'd charge it, and then reimburse him.

Twenty minutes later, armed with her purchases, Melissa found herself back in the warm sunshine on Wilshire Boulevard. She was bubbling over with the excitement of owning her first mink coat—or half-mink to be strictly accurate—and to celebrate she decided to treat herself to lunch at Jimmy's. Beverly Hills abounded with famous restaurants, but this was one of the few Rick had not taken her to.

But securing a table was easier said than done, and two champagne cocktails later, she was still hanging around the bar waiting for her name to be called.

'Hello.' She felt a tap on her shoulder, and with a start looked up to see Bart Huntingdon.

'Hi.' She gave him a friendly smile. 'Are you just arriving or leaving?'

'Luckily for you, arriving,' he replied drily, observing the two empty glasses on the table in front of her. 'I can see you've already been waiting some time, and if I don't rescue you, you'll be *non compos mentis* before they finally give you a table. I have a regular one by the window,' he added. 'Ideal for star-spotting, if that's your reason for being here.'

'That's awfully nice of you, but I don't want to barge in . . . I mean interrupt . . . if you're having a business lunch, or anything like that.' For some reason his offer was making her tongue-tied and awkward.

'I'm on my own,' he told her. 'Now if you'll allow me to rid you of all those interesting-looking packages, you can collect them from the cloakroom on the way out.'

'Are you sure they'll be safe?' she enquired anxiously.

'Why—what have you got in there? A mink coat?' he asked facetiously.

'As it happens—yes,' she answered, to his obvious surprise.

But he quickly recovered. 'Don't worry. They're two a penny in this town, and the attendant's probably got a couple herself,' he told her smoothly. 'She's an exceptionally pretty girl too.'

The implication was unmistakable, and Melissa itched to slap the complacent face.

'I bought it with my own money,' she informed him icily.

'Then you obviously earn more than any of *my* secretaries,' he answered drily. 'Frankly though, I'm not in the least interested in the whys and wherefores of your coat, but only in whether you intend trusting the hat-check girl with it. I'm hungry, and I don't want to stand around debating the point for another five minutes.'

It was not the most gracious invitation she'd ever received, but to refuse now would look childish. She'd lunch with him and prove she didn't give a hang what he thought of her, or her morals, as it was pretty clear that it was her supposed relationship with Rick that was bothering him. As a waiter disappeared with her parcels, and Melissa followed Bart to his table, she wondered why. Could it be some kind of protective attitude towards Jessica? Knowing her desire for a reconciliation, had he hoped to achieve it by having them both under the same roof? It was a thought that had occurred to Melissa earlier, and Bart's behaviour towards her tended to confirm it.

'Care for an aperitif?' Bart offered, as he sat down next to her on the banquette.

'No thanks.'

'You'll join me in some wine, though?'

'Perhaps one glass,' she relented.

The *Maître d'* appeared with the menus, and a short silence ensued while they chose their meal.

'Your usual wine, Mr Huntingdon?' the man enquired, after they'd both ordered grilled steaks for their main course.

Bart assented, but it was not until the waiter left that he enquired, 'You do drink red, don't you?'

Melissa nodded, slightly irritated that he'd not even bothered to note her preference before. But then he never poured wine himself at meals, and his attention towards her had verged on the perfunctory.

'I thought you might have gone for a steak with a sauce,' Melissa commented as her lone Caesar salad arrived, Bart having refused a first course.

'I prefer to stick to plain food at lunchtime.'

'Do you always lunch alone?'

'Never—but my date for today cancelled at the last moment.' He didn't bother to explain if it had been business or personal.

'But you always eat here?'

'What makes you think that?'

Oh boy, Melissa thought to herself. Trying to make conversation was an uphill struggle, or was he deliberately being difficult?

'You said you had a regular table, so naturally I assumed you ate here every day.'

'I enjoy their food, but I'm not devoted to it exclusively. They always keep my reservation until two, and if I'm not here by then, they give it to someone else.'

Well, that had just about exhausted *that* topic! Melissa racked her brain for something else to say. It was an unusual experience for her, but this man inhibited her as no other had ever done before.

'Is your office nearby?' Not exactly brilliant, but better than staring moronically into space.

'Ten minutes or so by car. If you're going straight back to the house after lunch, my chauffeur will take you,' he added.

'Thanks, but I'm not. I've heard so much about Rodeo Drive, I thought I'd window-shop this afternoon.'

'Is that how you spend your spare time in London as well?'

'Good lord, no! I usually get bored looking around shops unless it's with the intention of buying something. But somehow it's always different on holiday—even a working one like this.'

'Do you always accompany Rick?'

'This is the first time.' Melissa wondered if he were going to question her further about her relationship with the actor, but if he was curious, he was far too sophisticated to attempt anything so obvious.

'You're pretty enough to be in the profession yourself. Any ambitions along those lines?'

It was the first compliment he'd paid her, but uttered so prosaically it could hardly be regarded as flattery, merely a statement of fact.

'None. I'm fascinated by the talent and creativity of film-making, and even a little by the gloss, but that's as far as it goes.'

'You've landed yourself with the perfect job then,' he commented. 'How did you get it?'

Melissa waited until the waiter had finished serving the vegetables before replying.

'Through a friend.' She cut into her steak. It was just as she'd ordered it, medium rare. 'Her father's a theatrical costumier, and he's worked on several films with Rick.'

'What did you do before?'

'Worked for a solicitor.'

He nodded. 'Why did you leave? Not enough glamour and excitement?'

'Something like that,' she answered coolly. Irritated by the implied criticism, she didn't bother to explain that the real reason had been the ending of a relationship with one of the partners, and the awkwardness of coming into contact with him each day. 'But I don't regard it as a crime.'

He raised one well-formed eyebrow quizzically. 'I'm not aware I suggested it was.'

'You certainly gave that impression.' She sipped at her wine, a beautifully balanced Pinot

Noir. But even Monterey's finest couldn't soothe her rising anger.

He shrugged. 'In that case I apologise.' He motioned the waiter to clear away their plates. 'Would you like dessert?'

Melissa would have loved one, as she'd noticed several delicious concoctions on their way to other tables. But the idea of spending a moment longer than need be in the company of this boorish man made her refuse—particularly as he'd made no attempt to hide the fact that he didn't exactly find *her* company scintillating either.

'I don't want coffee myself, but you're welcome to some if you wish,' he offered politely.

'I'd rather be on my way. I'm sure you've a busy afternoon ahead of you too.'

'Not particularly,' he answered surprisingly. 'In fact, I'm playing tennis at a friend's. Paul Stewart and John Douglas are staying with him, and they're going to give us a few tips.' He named the Wimbledon and United States men's doubles champions for the past three years.

'You must be pretty good already,' she commented, 'or you wouldn't even have the nerve to knock up with them!'

For the first time he smiled. He was a deeper bronze than when they had first met, and it made his teeth appear brilliantly white.

'You obviously haven't seen me play!' He paused, and for a moment she wondered if he was going to ask her to do so. But he didn't. Instead he motioned for the bill. 'I'll drop you off at Rodeo Drive,' he said, as he checked it carefully, added a more than generous tip, then signed his name.

He was on friendly terms with all the staff, and it was clear from the smiles and exchanges of easy banter as they made their way out that he was a favourite customer. In spite of his immense wealth, he was not in the least condescending, and during the meal she'd noticed how he'd treated even the lowly commis boys as equals.

'Unless you've anything that's likely to melt in there,' Bart indicated her packages being placed in the boot of his Camargue by his chauffeur, 'it might be a good idea to let me take them back for you. If you're tempted to do more than window-shop, you'll have difficulty managing.'

'After this morning's extravagance that's unlikely,' she smiled. 'And really, I'd sooner not trouble you.' It was foolish, perhaps, but she was reluctant to allow her mink coat out of her sight.

But an hour later, as she strolled along Rodeo Drive in the sweltering hot afternoon sunshine, she cursed her obduracy. The dress and coat were in separate large boxes, and although they had handles, were difficult to hold comfortably for any length of time, and once again she stopped to interchange them from one hand to another. The shops were really fabulous, and the street lived up to its reputation as one of the finest in the world, but the price of anything that took her eye was prohibitive, and after another twenty minutes she finally concluded she'd had enough—for today at least. The pavements were crowded, and she stood at the edge, searching the busy road for a cab.

On the other side a yellow monster cruised slowly along, and Melissa hailed it, hurrying across before someone else grabbed it, dodging the oncoming cars as best she could.

'Where to?' the young driver asked.

Melissa gave him the adress and he nodded.

'Yeah. I've been up there before. It's the Huntingdon place, isn't it?'

'That's right.'

With a sigh of relief she relaxed against the leather of the Oldsmobile's back seat. All the windows were open and a pleasant, warm breeze soon restored her flagging spirits. Their route took them through some of Beverly Hills' loveliest streets, where each house was different from its neighbour, and where no car lowlier than a Jaguar was parked in the driveway. This was indeed Lotus Land, and whatever its detractors might say, it had plenty going for it.

Surprisingly, the man at the wheel was not particularly communicative, and ignored most of Melissa's attempts at conversation. He'd probably been driving all day and was tired, she sympathised. The constant heat was debilitating, and without air-conditioning, the eighty-five-degree temperature was enough to try the patience of a saint, apart from any hassle from his customers. Still, it was the first surly driver she'd come across. Previously she'd not only had a running commentary on which house belonged to what famous personality, but an estimate of their incomes, and the cabby's opinion of them too!

As they left the main residential area the traffic thinned, and before long they were the only car on the overgrown, tortuously twisting road that led to the Huntingdons' hilltop estate. In the driving mirror, Melissa caught the young man's gaze, and the look she saw there gave her a sudden feeling of foreboding. A moment later, as he brought the car to an abrupt halt, she knew her senses had not played her false.

'Get out,' he ordered, 'and leave everything, including your purse, in the cab.'

She did not attempt to argue with him, but just prayed his intention was only to rob her.

He climbed out after her, and she watched him empty the Neiman Marcus bags on to the back seat, and then riffle through her handbag.

'Is this all the cash you've got?' He held up the five twenty-dollar bills with disgust.

'Yes. I'm afraid——'

'Shut up.'

He leaned against the cab, and stared at her menacingly, thin-lipped, shifty-eyed, and sorely in need of a shave. Why hadn't she noticed all this before?

'Give me your watch and that gold locket round your neck,' he ordered. 'Then strip.'

Melissa resisted the urge to turn tail and run. He was wiry-looking, and besides, he had the car. How far could she get? And her attempt at flight might anger him enough to kill her. He hadn't produced a gun or a knife, but that was no guarantee he didn't have them.

Slowly she began to undo the buttons of her dress, her fingers trembling so much that it took some time to get each one through its hole.

'Hurry up,' he said impatiently. 'Or I'll rip it off you.'

'There's no need—I'm on the last one.' Melissa barely recognised the thin thread of sound as her own voice.

He came towards her, and instinctively she

backed away. But another couple of steps would take her over the edge, she realised, and whatever he intended doing with her, short of murder, was better than a fall of a hundred feet or so into the ravine below.

Melissa closed her eyes, and the sour stench of tobacco and bad breath assailed her nostrils. Then hot hands moved intimately over her body and a wave of nausea swept over her. She stifled the scream that threatened, frightened it might excite him to violence.

'Please,' she begged, opening her eyes and forcing herself to look him squarely in the face. 'Please leave me alone. I promise I won't tell the police about you. Just take my things and go.'

'You won't tell the cops anyway,' he said softly.

As his fingers touched the top of her lace briefs, Melissa made her move, and with panic-induced bravery, pushed her knee hard into his groin.

She heard him groan as he doubled up and clutched himself. Then she began to run. Heart pounding, mouth dry, she sped along the road, heedless of the fact she was barefooted, and it was not until she trod on a sharp stone and began to bleed that she cursed herself for taking off her shoes when she'd first entered the taxi.

Each step was now filled with pain, but still she did not slow her pace, for now she could hear her assailant behind her, breath rasping in his effort to catch her.

'Rich bitch,' she heard him say, followed by a string of filthy oaths.

Moments later he had an arm about her neck, and was swinging her round to face him.

'Filthy, rotten whore,' he said viciously.

Melissa saw the blow coming, and tried to dodge it. But he was too fast for her. His fist smashed violently into her face, there was a flash of agonising pain, then total oblivion.

CHAPTER FOUR

MELISSA'S lids opened and she stared at the fluffy white mass gathered above her. How pretty it was . . . It reminded her of clouds . . . She blinked her eyes. Was that what it was? Could she be in heaven, floating on a sea of cloud? She turned her head, and what was clearly French windows and blue sky beyond reassured her that wherever she was, it was not yet with her Maker. Then where on earth was she? She tried to think, but the harder she concentrated the more confused her brain became. Perhaps if she sat up it would help to get her bearings. Gingerly she attempted it, but although she knew she was moving, there was no feeling in her body. Was she partially paralysed? Could this account for the numbness and lack of co-ordination of her limbs? An icy blast of fear gripped her, threatening her sanity. She tried to banish the idea from her head, but could not contain a cry of anguish from her lips.

The sound immediately brought someone to her side. A girl of about her own age dressed in white. An angel of mercy, rather than a celestial one. It was a nurse, and her face bore an expression of relief.

'So you've finally come to. How are you feeling?'

'Terrible.' Melissa's voice was a croak, and barely discernible.

The nurse touched her comfortingly on the shoulder. 'A drink will ease your throat and make you sound less like a frog,' she said brightly and, lifting Melissa's head slightly, held a glass to her mouth, though she only allowed tiny sips.

'Is that better?' the girl asked, when Melissa had drunk her fill.

'A little,' she answered, then sank back against the pillows, tired from the effort. 'I feel such a fool. I can't remember where I am.'

'At Mr. Huntingdon's home, in Los Angeles.'

Of course. Now she realised her mistake. What she'd taken for a white cloud had been the pleated silk above her four-poster. As this thought came into her head, so did total recall.

'That man!' she cried, and struggled to sit up. 'That man who attacked me!'

But firm hands restrained her.

'Now, now, honey, you try to sleep again. There's nothing to worry about. It's all taken care of.'

'Taken care of?' Melissa's eyes widened, the aquamarine irises darkening with fear. 'Have they caught him? Tell me, have they caught him?'

'Yes, yes.' She felt cool fingers soothing her brow. 'Close your eyes now, and stop worrying.'

Melissa wanted to argue, but didn't have the strength. Perhaps if she could sleep again she'd feel well enough when she woke to ask all the questions tumbling through her mind. She closed her eyes, and long, thick lashes shaded the bruises beneath.

It was much later in the day when she opened her eyes again, aware of the difference in time because outside the window the sky was no longer bright blue but a deeper one as it began to fade into dusk. But she felt no better. In fact, considerably worse, as now she was aware of a soreness all over her body, as if she'd been used as a punching bag. Her face, too, when she tentatively put her fingers to it, was tender, and obviously very swollen.

She struggled to sit up in spite of the pain. In the dark shadows beyond the bed a woman stood up, and moved towards her. She too was dressed as a nurse, but was considerably older than the first.

'Feeling better now?' she enquired.

'Worse. Every part of my body aches.'

'I'm afraid you've had rather a bad time of it. Nothing serious,' she reassured Melissa when she saw her alarm. 'Just some cuts and very bad bruising. Your assailant beat you up pretty badly.'

Melissa's fingers clutched the sheets. 'They've caught him, though?'

The woman shook her head. 'Not yet.'

'But the other nurse said——'

'She wanted to calm you down. But don't worry, they'll get him. Mr Huntingdon's a very influential man, and because of it you can be assured the police will treat your case as special and give it priority.' The nurse placed a reassuring hand on Melissa's. 'I promised to tell the doctor the moment you were awake. Lie quietly, and I'll be back in a moment.'

She hurried out and Melissa obeyed. The conversation, though short, had exhausted her, and the room began to spin alarmingly. She felt as though she were in a whirlpool, being dragged round and round, and she struggled to raise her head so that she wouldn't be drawn into its vortex.

'Good evening, young lady.' The quiet words brought back a sense of reality, and as the room stopped revolving, Melissa was able to concentrate on the man who had spoken to her.

'Good evening,' she managed. 'Are you the doctor?'

'Yes.' He smiled down at her. 'The name's Bill Goldstein.'

He was a man of about forty-five, broad-framed and bulky, with receding brown hair, and a finely lined face.

'I'm the Huntingdons' family doctor when they're in Los Angeles,' he went on, 'and I've been taking care of you since Bart found you lying in the road three days ago.'

'You mean I've been unconscious for three days?' Her voice was high and shaky.

'I knocked you out with some pethidine to get you over the worst. You were pretty badly beat up, you know. Whoever the guy was, he needs psychiatric help as much as anything else.'

The memory of her ordeal swept over her, and involuntarily she shuddered.

'Did . . . did he . . . was I——?' Melissa stopped, unable to voice her fears.

'No, you weren't raped,' Bill Goldstein assured her, perceptively understanding what she had meant. 'The police's guess is that he got his kicks from hitting you, and then took off.' He patted her arm. 'They'll want to speak to you as soon as you feel up to it.'

'If delay means they'll have less chance of finding him, I'll talk to them now,' she said fiercely.

'We'll see,' he soothed. 'Let me take a look at you first.'

Melissa lay with her eyes closed as the doctor examined her. By the time he said there was nothing to worry about and that she could get out of bed if she felt up to it, she could barely open them again.

She touched her hand to her head. 'It's a strange feeling to have lost three days of your life. I can't remember a damned thing.'

'You might, eventually. But don't worry about it. They were three days best forgotten.'

There was a tap on the door.

'I think it's Mr Huntingdon.' The nurse addressed Bill Goldstein. 'He said to let him know as soon as you'd finished examining Miss Abbot. You know how anxious he's been.'

'I'd like to see him,' Melissa said.

The door opened, and Bart came into the room, dominating it with his presence, very much as he had the restaurant when she'd lunched with him at Jimmy's. Was that only three days ago? Good grief! The normality of it seemed like a lifetime away.

'Not exactly a pretty sight,' he greeted her with a warm smile. 'But one hell of a lot better than when I first saw you lying in the roadway.' Sherry-brown eyes twinkled down at her. 'For a moment you had Gus and me really worried. We thought you were dead.'

'The way I feel at the moment, it might have been preferable.'

'Don't start feeling sorry for yourself.' This

from Bill Goldstein, in a firm, no-nonsense doctor's voice. 'Think positive. You'll recover one hell of a lot quicker.'

'Leave her to me, Bill,' Bart told him. 'I'll have her on the tennis courts playing mixed doubles by the end of the week.'

'From a wheelchair!' Melissa quipped, but could not quite rustle up the energy to accompany it with a smile.

Telling her he'd be in to see her again the following morning, the doctor departed, and tactfully the nurse withdrew, leaving her alone with Bart.

'Are there any leads on my attacker?' Melissa asked at once.

'Not really,' he answered regretfully. 'But once you give the police a description of him, and look through some mug shots, that will be a big help. They found the cab abandoned downtown. Wiped clean of finger-prints, of course. And he'd stolen it too. If you'd only thought to check your guy's face against the photograph of the real driver in the front of the cab.'

'If I'd only noticed how shifty-looking my man was in the first place, I'd never have got into it!' she replied.

'I guess not. It's easy to be clever *after* the event, isn't it?' he commented whimsically.

There was a tap on the door, and the nurse put her head round.

'Sorry to intrude, but Mr. Rayburn's on the line from Las Vegas, asking to speak to Miss Abbot.'

Melissa drew a deep breath and pressed her hands to her eyes. She'd completely forgotten she was supposed to be there with Rick. How would he make out without her?

'He was extremely reluctant to leave you, but I insisted,' Bart cut across her thoughts. 'You've been quite ill, Melissa, but not ill enough to warrant a half-million-dollar delay in the shooting schedule. That's why I stayed instead. Things seem to be running fairly smoothly with Rick and Jessica, so I decided it was worth the risk of leaving them to their own devices for a while.'

He who pays the piper calls the tune, Melissa thought wryly, and it must have galled Rick to have been forced to dance to it—but unless a delay was caused through his own illness, he could be sued for breach of contract.

'I'd like to speak to him,' she said aloud, and reached for the phone by the side of the bed.

'Would you like me to leave?' Bart asked.

'Not at all,' she answered, as she placed it to her ear and said hello.

'Melissa, sweetheart, you sound lousy.' Rick's distinct voice could easily be heard by Bart, seated on a chair beside her bed.

'I don't exactly feel great either!'

'I miss you, darling. If that cold bastard hadn't insisted I'd never have left you. You know that, don't you?'

'Of course.' Deliberately she closed her eyes, aware that Bart must have overheard, and embarrassed to meet his gaze. 'Anyway, I'm in good hands, and Bart's doctor has assured me I'll be up and about in a few days.'

'Don't worry about the dress and mink coat,' Rick said. 'I've already settled the bill. You can go to Neiman Marcus any time and replace them.'

She didn't have the strength to go through the rigmarole of explaining that she was paying for the coat herself, and she'd be responsible for its loss.

'That's sweet of you,' she said instead. 'We'll discuss it when I see you.'

'It looks as if we'll be here for at least a couple of weeks. So you get better quickly, darling, and fly out here as soon as you feel up to it.' There was a loud noise, approximating a kiss. 'I'll be in touch again tomorrow.'

Gently Bart took the receiver from her hand and replaced it. 'I think you've had enough talking for one night,' he said, and stood up.

How tall he appeared towering over her, and how powerful-looking too, in spite of his slim build. But then his shoulders were surprisingly broad. He had loosened his tie, and undone the top button of his shirt. It gave him a sensual air, and she averted her eyes from the soft tangle of dark hair that she glimpsed at the base of his throat. With such thoughts, she couldn't be quite as ill as she'd imagined!

'You've been very kind,' she murmured. 'The nurses . . . your doctor . . . Thank you.'

'Kind?' he said, with sudden irritation. 'What did you expect me to do? Put you in the pauper's ward of a public hospital?'

For some unknown reason his reprimand made her feel like bursting into tears. It must be shock, and the drugs she'd been given, Melissa decided. Her system was naturally weakened, and the slightest thing could upset her.

'I'm leaving for San Diego early in the morning, so I won't disturb you.' Bart was speaking again. 'Nurse Fuller will be staying the night, though, and she'll tell me how you are before I go. But I'll be back in the evening, and if you're feeling up to it, perhaps we might have dinner together.'

He smiled at her, and she smiled back, and then he left her alone.

Alone. It was odd how frightening that could be, even though it was only for a few minutes. But there was no doubting her relief when the night nurse re-appeared to take her mind off the memory of her attack, and reassure her with the cheerful sick-room patter that was her stock-in-trade.

Next morning Melissa was allowed to get out of bed, and had the shock of her life when she first saw herself in the bathroom mirror. Her face and body were a mass of angry-looking bruises, some in more violent hues than others.

And to think Bart had seen her like this, she mused, as she lowered herself into the warm, scented water, relaxing as the nurse gently began to bathe her with a soft flannel. She'd been near-naked when she'd fled her attacker, and for all the covering her bikini-briefs afforded, she might as well have been completely nude.

Bart's chauffeur had also been with him when he'd found her lying in the road, though somehow this thought didn't disturb her anywhere near as much. In any case, it was not her lack of clothing that bothered her—she'd gone topless too many times on holiday to be embarrassed by the exposure of her body. No, it was the knowledge that she looked so horrifically ugly and distorted.

Yet why should she care how she appeared to Bart? True, she found him attractive—but what girl in her right mind wouldn't? Intelligent too, although she knew this from what she'd overheard him say, rather than from his sparkling conversation with *her*! Their lunch was a good example of his stilted manner whenever they'd found themselves alone. Until now, of course. But that meant nothing.

'How do you feel now?' the nurse was asking, as she dabbed Melissa dry with a soft towel. 'Well enough to sit out on your terrace?'

Melissa nodded and the woman settled her comfortably on the luxuriously padded easy-chair. Melissa closed her eyes, somewhat alarmed at how shaky she felt, and how quickly she'd grown tired. Too tired to have dinner with Bart that night, in fact, or for the next two either, though he was a constant visitor to her room. As were the detectives who came to question her. She spent a good deal of time looking at photographs of known criminals in the hope she could identify her assailant, but when she failed to do so, a police artist arrived to do a photo-fit composite. Although robbery with violence was a routine occurrence, as her night nurse had predicted, because of Bart's influential position no effort was being spared to track down her attacker.

By the end of the week she was considerably stronger, and on Saturday was able to spend the day by the pool.

'Try and eat a bit more, even if you have to force it down,' Bill Goldstein instructed, when he arrived to give her her morning check-up. 'If you don't, I'll be able to use you as a demonstration skeleton at one of my classes!'

She thought of this when she put on her

swimsuit, and examined herself in the cheval mirror before leaving her room. Her collarbones protruded sharply, and the thinness of her body made her breasts look fuller. Well, at least the bruises were fading, and most of the swelling had gone down, although her eyes and mouth were still a bit puffy, so make-up was definitely out. Donning a pair of large-framed sunglasses, that hid most of her face, and wishing her brief bikini did the same to her figure, she made her way to the pool.

Hardly had she seated herself, when Bart sauntered into sight, coolly appraising her from head to toe.

Melissa did the same to him, though with her eyes hidden behind her sunglasses she could do it without the same degree of obviousness. She'd not seen him so briefly clad before, and found that in the flesh he was, if anything, dishier than in clothes. His shoulders were wider than she'd supposed, his stomach flat, his legs long and lean and curving down to strong-looking calves. The tangle of hair she'd glimpsed on his chest the other night was thick, and as dark as his brows, with not a grey hair in sight.

'Are you well enough to swim?' he asked. 'Or are you dressed like that just to show off your new slimline figure?'

Well, so he had noticed what it was like before!

'I was a bit nervous going in on my own,' she answered. 'But now you're here I think I will.'

'Good.' He performed a perfect swallow dive, then returned at a fast crawl to the near end where she was still seated.

'How about it?' he called.

Not yet feeling energetic enough to dive in, Melissa entered by way of the steps and, considerately, Bart slowed down his own pace to keep level with her. But by the time she'd executed a couple of lengths she was breathless.

'The last time I was in, I did ten lengths,' she commented as she levered herself out to sit on the edge. 'I'll have to build up day by day,' she added, squeezing the water from her hair.

'It's a wonderful colour.' Bart touched the red-gold plait with his hand. It was a beautiful hand, with slim, hard fingers and very strong muscles. 'I'd often wondered if it was real, but now I know it is.'

She had no need to ask how.

'What about *your* hair?' she asked to hide her sudden shyness, though there had been nothing suggestive in his tone to cause it. He could not have been more prosaic, in fact.

'It's not dyed either,' he said in an amused voice.

'I didn't mean that,' she smiled. 'When did it turn grey?'

'At college,' he answered surprisingly. 'But it's a family trait. My mother was completely grey by the time she was twenty-three. She coloured her hair, though, back to its original chestnut—and still does to this day.'

'I don't blame her. It may give character to a man, but it's horribly ageing on a woman.'

'It's certainly never bothered *me*,' he said. 'And to my parents' delight it stopped me going through the phase of moustaches and beards to make myself look older than my age. I always did!'

'I don't agree. I was fooled the first time I saw

you from a distance playing with one of the Great Danes, but close to it was obvious you weren't in your dotage!'

'Compared to you I am,' he replied. 'But then so is Rick. Clearly you like older men.'

'I wasn't aware I'd said I liked *you*,' she snapped.

She waited for a comment, but when he made none she busied herself plumping up the cushions on her sunbed, before lying down on it again and spreading out her hair to dry.

'It's sizzling.' Bart touched a damp strand. 'But then, with your colouring, I imagine it's not the only part of you that boils over fairly quickly!'

Except for a fleeting smile she ignored the remark, and watched while he settled on the sun-bed next to her.

'Perhaps that's why *I* like *you*,' he continued. 'Whatever your relationship with Rick, it's a down-to-earth one, and you're not frightened to tell him what you think.'

It wasn't exactly an apology for his previous remark, but coming from him it was as near as she could hope for.

'I've had to take care of myself since I was thirteen,' she replied. 'I suppose that's made me very much my own person.'

'Was that how old you were when your parents died?' She nodded and he went on, 'Rick told me they were killed in an avalanche.'

Did that mean he'd been interested enough in her to question Rick about her background? Perhaps. But it would be foolish to put too important an interpretation on it, when it was probably little more than common curiosity.

'My only consolation is that at least they died together. They were extremely devoted, and it was the way they would have chosen,' she told him aloud.

'What happened afterwards? Were you taken in by relatives or did you have to go to an orphanage?'

Her parents' generous donations had more or less kept their local one afloat! But Melissa had no intention of telling Bart this.

'Two of my uncles managed to scrape enough money together to send me to boarding school,' she answered, with a well-practised lie. It was the one she always used to explain away her expensive education. 'They're bachelors, and having a young child around made them uneasy. It was worth anything to them to get rid of me.'

'You don't sound particularly angry about it,' he remarked with surprise.

'I was fortunate in the school they chose,' she explained truthfully. 'I made a lot of good friends there, most of whom I still see.'

'What about the uncles?'

'We exchange Christmas cards!'

He chuckled. 'Say no more!'

'What about *your* childhood?' Melissa asked. 'Obviously you didn't go to boarding school like me.'

He raised an eyebrow quizzically. 'Why obviously?'

'I thought Americans were too democratic to believe in the élitism of private education.'

'Most are,' he agreed. 'But my parents are among the few who prefer it.'

'You mean the rich few, don't you?'

He shrugged.

'Where did you go?' she persisted.

'Groton, Princeton, then two years at the Sorbonne.'

'Did you enjoy living in Paris?'

'What red-blooded American boy wouldn't?'

'I rather had the impression *yours* was blue!' Because he seemed so relaxed, Melissa thought she'd see how he reacted to being teased.

'You mean you think I'm a snob?' He lowered his head and their eyes met. 'My dislike of Rick has nothing to do with his working-class background.'

Back to square one again, she thought, where all roads led to Rick.

'He treated Jessica pretty badly, and she almost had a breakdown when he divorced her,' he continued. 'And of course coming here and flaunting you in her face was hardly the most tactful thing to do.'

'They've been divorced for several years, and I'm sure she doesn't think he's been leading the life of a monk, so why should *he* have to do so just because they're making a film together?' Melissa undid the halter strap of her top. 'Are you protective towards her because she's a friend, or because you're in love with her yourself?'

His lips tightened. 'You certainly don't beat about the bush, do you?'

'I thought that was the thing you liked about me,' she said artlessly.

'It is.' He gave a wry smile. 'But I prefer it when your honesty is directed at someone else!'

'I'm surprised *you're* honest enough to admit it!'

'What else could I do?' he chuckled. 'You had me over a barrel.'

He still hadn't answered her question, but she decided to leave it for the moment. With a sigh she closed her eyes again. The heat from the sun enveloped her, bringing with it a pleasing lethargy, and it was easy to forget everything except the luxury of her surroundings. Melissa fell into a deep slumber, and when she awoke was surprised to find she'd been asleep for nearly an hour.

She sat up and stretched, and only then became aware that Bart was still beside her. He too had dozed off, and she noticed how much younger he looked with his features completely relaxed. His head had fallen slightly to one side, and he hadn't bothered to comb his hair, but had allowed it to dry in the sun. It had an unruly look to it, making him appear carefree and somehow vulnerable. It was a way she had never thought of him before, and she could see the danger in doing so. He was a man never to be under-estimated or taken for granted.

He murmured something undiscernible, and shifted his body so that he was now facing her. He was breathing deeply, and exuded a warmth that made her extremely physically conscious of him. She felt an uncontrollable urge to touch him, but as she put out her hand to do so, his eyes suddenly opened. Sherry-brown, they appeared fathomless, and she was reminded of a warm, deep pool, tempting her to its very depth, to encompass her, embrace her, never let her go. Now what had made that fanciful notion pop into her head? Confused, she banished it, and instead concentrated her attention on her hair.

'Don't re-plait it,' he said, putting out a hand to restrain her 'You look like a mermaid.'

'A schoolgirl would be more apt,' she smiled.

'What's wrong with that? Most women would envy you.'

She sighed. 'I guess no one's ever happy with their own image.'

'You've less reason than most to complain,' he smiled.

'Thank you,' she said pertly. 'But I wasn't looking for a compliment.'

'I know. That's why I paid you one.' He swung long legs over the side of his chair and stood up. 'Do you feel up to another swim before lunch?' he asked. 'Or have you had enough?'

'I think I'll wait until this afternoon.'

'Then so will I. I needed an excuse to be really lazy, and keeping you company is as good as any!'

They ate beneath a three-sided pavilion near the pool. It was covered with flowering creepers, and high-level windows allowed soft sunlight, filtered by the plants, into the interior. There were no long silences as there had been the previous time they'd lunched alone, and Melissa found he could be an amusing raconteur when he wished. More amusing than Rick, whose way with a story she had always admired. But Bart's sense of fun was keener, his intellect sharper, and he brought his anecdotes to life with sophisticated panache. Because of the relaxed atmosphere, she asked him a question she might otherwise not have attempted.

'You've been brought up in such a rarefied and privileged environment,' she said. 'Don't you feel it's stopped you from knowing what the *real* world is all about?'

'Rarefied and privileged perhaps, but not ignorant,' he answered after a moment's thought. 'Although I can't claim to have known hardship and poverty first hand, it's something I'm not blind to. A social conscience was something my parents instilled in all their children, and in our own way we do our best to help those who need it.' He toyed with the stem of his wine-glass. 'I hope that doesn't sound smug or boastful. It wasn't meant to.'

She shook her head. 'No ambition for politics *à la* Kennedys, though?' she asked. 'I mean as a way of helping other than money?'

'No—it's a power that's never interested me.'

'Too much sucking up to people to reach the top?' she smiled.

'Too much sucking up to the *wrong* kind of people to reach the top,' he corrected. 'The kind I despise, but who would have to be repaid for their help.'

'So instead you followed in your father's footsteps,' she commented.

'That was entirely my own choice.' He sipped his white wine appreciatively. It was his family's own label. 'And one I've never regretted, Melissa.'

His glance was warm, and as she basked in its glow she suddenly wondered how he would have reacted to her if they had met under different circumstances? As equals, for example. Would he have asked her out? More to the point, would she have accepted his invitation? Without doubt, she admitted with her usual honesty. He was the most intriguing man she'd ever met. The most sexually exciting, too. Yet, unlike most others, he didn't set out to captivate. Quite the opposite. His attraction stemmed from his *laissez-faire* attitude.

'I wish I was a mind reader.' His voice cut across her thoughts. 'You have such a rapt look on your face, your thoughts must be very interesting.'

'I was thinking that staying here with you is like being entertained in a Sultan's palace,' she improvised with a teasing glint in her eyes. 'Is that interesting enough for you?'

'Only if you see yourself as part of my harem!'

'Who wouldn't! I'm sure you're very generous to your favourites.'

'Do you need to be bought?' he asked casually.

Her remark had clearly been meant as a joke, yet Melissa sensed a serious overtone to his question.

'I don't think that requires an answer.'

He leaned back in his chair. 'Shall I interpret that as no?'

'Frankly I don't give a hang how you interpret it,' she said sharply. 'My morals are none of your business.'

'I'd like to make them mine though.'

'What's that supposed to mean?'

'It's quite simple. If your loyalty depends on your reward, I can offer far more than Rick.'

Melissa was furious. How dared he treat her like a common whore? No, not a common one, she corrected bitterly. A high-class one. He'd never allow himself to be interested in anything that was cheap.

'With friends like you, who needs enemies?' she snapped.

'I never professed to be Rick's friend,' he said flatly.

'Of course,' she retorted. 'It's poor lovelorn Jessica you're thinking of. With me out of Rick's hair, you think she'll be able to get him back, don't you?' It had taken some time before the actress had condescendingly asked Melissa to call her by her first name, and then it was only at her ex-husband's prompting.

'Would you believe me if I told you my interest in you has nothing to do with Rick or Jessica?'

'You mean you want me for myself alone?' she asked sarcastically.

'Why should you find that surprising?' he said soberly. 'Even bruised and battered you're easier on the eye than most other women on a *good* day.'

Melissa was too annoyed—no, why not be truthful, too disappointed—by his proposition to be flattered by the compliment.

'Thanks for the offer,' she answered coldly. 'But I prefer to stick with the devil I know rather than the devil I don't.'

'I'm sure my sexual proclivities are no more peculiar than Rick's,' he replied urbanely.

Melissa knew he'd deliberately misinterpreted what she'd said to provoke her further, though for what reason she wasn't sure. Some kind of admission, perhaps?

'I'll take your word for it,' she said, and flung down her napkin. 'Meanwhile you can swim on your own this afternoon, and I hope you damn well drown!'

As swiftly as she could she made her way back to the house, crossed the vast hall, then took the stairs in rapid succession to her bedroom.

Without pausing to catch her breath or have second thoughts, she pressed the bell to summon one of the servants, and when the man appeared a couple of minutes later, she asked him to call her a taxi.

'You're leaving?' he asked with surprise, noticing the open cases on her bed.

'Yes, I am.' She was in no mood to go into further explanations. 'Please let me know as soon as the taxi arrives.'

'It will be at least half an hour,' the swarthy-skinned man told her. Like most of the domestic staff, he was Mexican.

Higgledy-piggledy, she flung her clothes into the cases. If they creased what did it matter? They'd soon hang out, and those that didn't were easily pressed. It was a pity she'd have to leave her favourite nightdress behind, but it had been removed for laundering and wasn't yet back. One had only to leave the room for a few minutes and someone was in it tidying up, and collecting for washing any item that had been worn.

She heard the door open and swung round to see Bart coming towards her. He was wearing a towelling robe and his hair was still wet. Obviously he'd been in the pool when the houseman had gone down to inform him of her departure.

'Don't you usually knock before entering a lady's bedroom?' Melissa demanded angrily.

'It depends who the lady is, and the purpose of my visit,' he answered smoothly. 'And in this case I decided she probably wouldn't open it to me if I did.' He eyed the suitcases. 'Don't you think you're acting rather childishly?'

'I'll act whatever way suits me—and your opinion of my behaviour doesn't interest me in the slightest.'

He shrugged. 'Where do you intend to go? Las Vegas to join Rick?'

'Perhaps. I haven't decided.'

'Then I suggest you do before you leave. I don't think it's a very good idea for you to drive around Los Angeles without a place to stay—the hotels are still pretty full, and you might have difficulty finding a room.'

'I'll use your name,' she said sarcastically. 'I'm sure that will open all doors to me.'

She banged the case she was packing shut, and began on another.

'There's half a bra hanging out of the back,' Bart pointed out with unconcealed amusement in his voice.

'So what?'

'Don't you care if the world knows your cup size?' He moved a few steps closer. 'Thirty-four C,' he read aloud. 'You're quite a handful, Melissa, in more ways than one!'

'Very funny,' she said sarcastically. 'I think I prefer you when you're serious!'

'If you promise to stay, I'll promise not to make any more jokes.'

She stopped her packing and looked up at him. 'I'm touched by your concern for my well-being, but I'm quite able to look after myself.'

'You didn't do a very good job of it the other day,' he pointed out.

'Forewarned is forearmed,' she said with a toss of her head. 'I shan't allow anything like that to happen to me again.'

'Don't be over-confident. A girl on her own is always vulnerable.'

'I promise not to go out after dark? Does that satisfy you?' she said defiantly.

'No.' He looked at her from narrowed eyes. 'With Rick away I feel responsible for you, and if you're not going directly to him, you'll stay here.'

'Don't be so ridiculous. You can't stop me leaving.'

'Can't I?' With swift strides he was at the door, removing the key. 'When you're ready to behave like an adult, just ring the bell.' Before she could protest further, he'd closed the door behind him, and she heard the key turning in the lock outside.

Angry and frustrated, she banged her hands against the door, wishing it was Bart Huntingdon's head.

'Let me out of here or I'll call the police!' she cried.

'And what will you tell them?' he asked with maddening calm.

'That you're holding me against my will. In our country that's called abduction, and carries a pretty heavy prison sentence.'

'You don't think they'll believe you, do you?' Although she couldn't see him, Melissa knew he was smiling.

'Not everyone's influenced by your money,' she shouted.

There was no reply, and she wondered if he was still there, but pride forbade her enquiring. Instead she sat down on her bed and buried her head in her hands.

What a fool he'd made of her. She knew she'd

lost this round—for the moment at least. Without his say-so, no car could leave or enter the grounds of the estate, and to attempt it on foot was an impossibility, even if she'd felt strong enough to try. And in any case, where would she walk *to*? There were no other houses nearby, and the only road down to Los Angeles was the one on which she'd been robbed and nearly raped. No way could she face that on her own, with or without her suitcases.

Melissa went into the bathroom and put a couple of soluble aspirins into a glass to soothe her pounding head. They sizzled like her own temper. She had no choice, so there was nothing to think over. She must stay here whether she liked it or not.

CHAPTER FIVE

ANTICIPATING some reference to his victory, Melissa was pleasantly surprised when she came down to dinner that evening and found Bart acting as if nothing had happened. Instead he was the concerned host and she a welcome guest. Because of it she made up her mind to forget her previous grievances, and enjoy his company.

'I thought it might be a good idea to take you to my beach house tomorrow,' he said during the meal. 'Of all my homes it's my favourite, and I'd like you to see it. The sea air will do you good as well.'

Melissa was pleased by his offer. Not just because she hadn't yet been to the ocean, but because she was curious to see what constituted his favourite home.

'I had it built three years ago,' he went on, 'and I spend most of my free time there.'

'Aren't you frightened I might run away?' she asked slyly.

He laughed. 'It's about as inaccessible as this place, so where would you run to?'

Melissa gave an exaggerated sigh. 'I can see I'll have to go back to my original plan of knotted sheets out of the window in the middle of the night!'

He laughed again. 'You're not still thinking of leaving, are you?'

'I guess not. I'll be fit enough to join Rick in Las Vegas in a few days, and this hotel's better than most to recuperate in. At least the rates are reasonable!'

'*And* you get to dine with the management!' he smiled.

'So far that hasn't been much of a bonus!'

'Am I such poor company?' One eyebrow quirked.

She shrugged. 'I'm sure you *can* be fun—but so far your charm hasn't exactly overwhelmed me!'

'You're referring to my suggestion this afternoon, of course,' he said perceptively.

'That didn't help.' She rested her knife and fork on her plate. 'If we're going to spend the whole of tomorrow together, I suggest we call a truce. You stop treating me as if I'm some kind of high-class call-girl on the make, and I'll try to think of you as I would any other attractive man who's asked me out for the day.'

He didn't attempt to deny her accusation. Instead, he leaned across the table and placed a lean, tanned hand on hers. 'Agreed,' he said softly.

Long after he had resumed eating, Melissa was still tinglingly aware of his touch. It had been casual enough, but sufficient to set her pulses racing. Perhaps spending a day alone with him at a lonely beach house wasn't such a good idea, she mused. There was no doubt she found him attractive and had it not been for Rick she wouldn't have gone to such pains to hide it from him. But then, she reminded herself, had there been no need for the pretence, she wouldn't have been here in the first place. Loyalty to her employer had made her keep Bart at arm's length until now, and she must continue to do so, however tempted she was to show how she really felt.

They were having coffee when the butler came in to inform her that Rick was on the line from Vegas. He had telephoned each day as well as sending fresh flowers, and it was difficult not to be touched by his concern. It was not entirely altruistic, she knew, but if his flowers and notes were part of the barricade against Jessica, his solicitude regarding her health was completely genuine.

'How's my girl?' he asked at once. 'Feeling better today?'

'Much,' she answered. 'I even managed a swim.' She went on to tell him that Bart had invited her out for the day, and that she might not be in when he rang the following night. 'How are things with Jessica?' she enquired softly, though she was well out of range of Bart's hearing.

'Difficult,' he answered briefly. 'But there haven't been any tantrums so far.'

'Still not succumbed to temptation?'

'With Jessica, or all the other leggy lovelies here?'

'Either,' Melissa laughed.

'Difficult as it is, I've been completely faithful to you, my darling,' he assured her. 'Though I have to say being celibate for so many weeks is the toughest role I've ever played!'

'Even when I join you I can't help you there.' Melissa reiterated her stance. His frustration was obviously reaching boiling point, and it might be a good idea to pour cold water over his hopes now.

When she returned to the dining-room, Bart was no longer there, and the table had been cleared except for her half-empty coffee cup.

'Mr Huntingdon had a call from Pittsburgh on one of the other lines,' a manservant informed her. 'He said it was going to take some time, and would you excuse him if he doesn't rejoin you?'

Although it was probably true, Melissa was piqued all the same, though she was careful not to show it.

'Did he mention anything about tomorrow?' she enquired.

'I was to ask you to be down by seven-thirty. The beach-house is quite a distance, even by plane, and Mr Huntingdon wants to make an early start.'

Melissa hadn't realised they would be flying, and was surprised Bart hadn't mentioned it. He'd probably intended to when she returned, but then had been called to the phone himself.

She made her way up to her room. She was not really sorry to have an early night. One way or another, today had been quite eventful, and with a long and even more tiring one ahead of her, the blandness of one of the showbiz chat shows on television, was suitably soporific—in direct contrast to Bart's company! In fact, within ten minutes of climbing into bed she was asleep—dream-racked hours from which she awoke unrefreshed, and with disturbing thoughts of Bart still uppermost in her mind.

He was already in the hall waiting for her

when she came downstairs, exactly to time.
Dressed completely in black, trousers, open-
necked silk shirt, and fine cashmere sweater,
knotted casually around his neck, he looked
intensely masculine.

'Will you excuse my triteness when I say you
look as pretty as a picture?' he said, taking her
beach bag from her, and stowing it in the boot
of his car. Not the Rolls, but another of the
innumerable makes he owned—though this time
she did not recognise the shape or the name.

'That depends on the picture,' she answered
pertly.

'Dressed in sugar-pink and white, what else
could it be but a Renoir?' he smiled, making no
attempt to hide his admiration.

Melissa was pleased at the compliment. After
a good deal of deliberation she'd chosen to wear
one of her new outfits, a pretty white and pink
cotton dress, with a shoestring-strapped bodice
embroidered with a motif, and a gold-trimmed
cord belt around the frilled, layered skirt. It
suited her even more now than it had in the
shop in London, for her skin was tanned, which
highlighted the red-gold of her hair. Today she
wore it loose around her shoulders, and she was
glad that in spite of the still visible bruises, she
had never looked prettier.

'No chauffeur?' she asked, as Bart closed the
door behind her, and climbed into the driving
seat.

'I enjoy driving myself for a change, and I'll
leave the car at the airport. We can collect it on
the way back.'

'But isn't Gus also your bodyguard?' asked
Melissa as they set off down the driveway.

'Unfortunately, yes. But I feel quite safe where I'm taking you, so I don't need him along.'

'And where is that?' she quizzed.

'You'll see when you get there. I want it to be a surprise.'

His mouth clamped firmly shut, and she could see it would be pointless to question him further. Instead she concentrated her attention on his driving. It was fast, but well under control, and he was careful not to exceed the speed limit, though he commented that he found it frustrating.

'What do you think of her?' Bart asked, after a while.

'Think of whom?'

He chuckled. 'The car, silly.'

'It goes,' she said offhandedly.

'I should damn well hope so! She was custom built and cost a small fortune.'

'That goes without saying.'

He ignored the sarcasm. 'Not me personally, but for a promotion for one of our companies. I liked it so much when I saw it, though, I decided to keep it for myself. Alan Clénet, the designer, has quite a business out here, and there's always a waiting list for his cars.'

He turned on to the highway that led to the airport, and for a while drove in silence.

'I must apologise for my disappearance last night.' He was the first to break it. 'I hope you didn't mind?'

'I was glad of an early night,' she answered. 'Though I didn't sleep too well, as it happens.'

'Troubled dreams?'

'No—indigestion,' she lied.

'It was probably that second helping of profiteroles,' he teased.

'Probably. But I was taking Bill Goldstein's advice and trying to fatten myself up.'

Bart glanced at her. 'Considering what you've been through, your looks don't pity you—whatever Bill says to the contrary, golden girl.'

'Golden girl'. Melissa repeated it to herself. It sounded almost like an endearment, and immediately she felt a warmth between them, that had not been there before.

'Do you think they'll ever catch the man who attacked me?' she asked.

'Frankly—no. The police are doing their best, and I've even put our top security man on it. But unless you actually see the guy again and recognise him, the description you gave could fit a thousand faces. The only hope is that when he tries to sell the coat it's reported.'

'Rather a forlorn hope, isn't it, given how most people love a bargain.'

'Do you?' he smiled.

'Not of the falling-off-the-back-of-a-lorry variety,' she answered. 'But when I see a sale sign, it's like red rag to a bull!'

Bart chuckled. 'I believe you. I've never heard you sound so fierce!'

'Hearing is nothing—you should see me in full charge on the first day of Harrods sale!'

He turned into the airport's entrance, but drove past the main building itself.

'Our plane's parked out on one of the far runways,' he told her. 'The nicest thing about having your own is that you don't have to hang around waiting for your flight to be called.'

It had not occurred to Melissa that they would be flying in a private aircraft, but that surprise was as nothing compared to the one she received when she saw the size of it. Expecting something comparatively small, like a Lear jet, she was faced instead with a Boeing 707.

'This is actually *yours*?' she asked in astonishment.

'Bought this year and fully paid for,' he said with deliberate nonchalance. 'But I only use it when I want to impress a special girl-friend!'

Melissa knew he was teasing. 'What do you use for the others?'

'Last year's model, naturally!'

'You sound just like a regular Hollywood hero!'

'I try,' he smiled.

A uniformed hostess greeted them at the top of the steps, and after settling Melissa into one of the numerous armchairs, Bart disappeared forward to speak to the Captain.

It gave Melissa a chance to take in her surroundings, which by any standards were luxurious, far more so than first class on an airline. Leather and suede armchairs and settees, in shades of beige and brown on a deep-pile cream carpet, were scattered with orange silk cushions that matched the walls, while the tables were of heavy, smoked perspex, as was the bar.

'I'll give you a conducted tour when we're airborne. There's an office, bedroom and bathroom as well,' Bart told her when he reappeared. 'But for the moment, fasten your seatbelt. We've just been cleared for take-off.'

'When do you intend telling me our destination?' Melissa enquired, as they began to gain height, and Los Angeles, in all its palm-tree and swimming-pool glory, began to take on the appearance of a toy town.

'How does Cap Ferrat sound to you?' Bart smiled.

'Fine,' Melissa laughed. 'But where are we going?'

'I've just told you—Cap Ferrat,' he repeated.

She searched his face for some kind of sign to indicate he was joking, but incredibly there was none.

'You invited me out for the *day*,' she said slowly, attempting to control her temper. 'Why did you lie to me?'

'Because I knew you wouldn't come with me if I told you the truth,' he said without apology. 'And I did want you to see my house.'

'Rubbish,' she said, tight-lipped. 'You knew I was going to join Rick in Las Vegas in a couple of days, and you wanted to stop me.' Heedless that the warning light was still on, she undid her safety belt and jumped up from her seat. 'I insist you have the plane turned round and take me back.'

'I admit I wanted to stop you, but the reason has nothing to do with Jessica,' he answered, completely ignoring her request. 'I've told you that before, but for some reason you refuse to believe me—though at least now it's obvious you no longer believe I'm in love with her myself.' His head tilted upwards, the hair glinting siver in the overhead lights. 'Don't you know I've wanted you from almost the first day we met, and that I haven't been able to get you out of my mind? God!' he swore, 'you've even come between me and my work.'

Amazed, Melissa stared at him, too stunned by his outburst to reply.

'Why the surprise?' he demanded. 'Surely you're aware of how desirable you are?'

'The world's full of desirable women—particularly your world,' she said coolly. 'What makes me so special?'

'Everything. The way you talk, the way you laugh, even the way you get angry . . . I enjoy being with you.'

'That hasn't always been very obvious,' she said drily.

'Only because I didn't want to show how I felt about you.' He stood up. 'You were Rick's girl, after all.'

'*Were?*' she questioned sharply. 'I still am.'

'Not for the next few days, Melissa. At the end of that time you can decide which of us you really want.' Deep-set sherry-brown eyes met her own aquamarine ones unwaveringly. 'Your loyalty to Rick is commendable, but I'm damn sure you're not in love with him, whatever his feelings for *you*.'

Clearly Rick's acting is more convincing than mine, Melissa thought, but then he was a professional after all, and more used to pretending emotions he didn't feel.

'I don't know how you can be so certain of that,' she answered aloud.

'You're too intelligent . . . too mature . . . too much your own person—you'd never play second fiddle to his ego.'

Obstinately Melissa refused to allow herself to be impressed by his words. However tempting it might be, her first loyalty was still to Rick, and she had to keep remembering it.

'The same could be said for Jessica—and *she* married him.'

'True.' Bart acknowledged the point. 'But it was also one of the reasons for the divorce. They had absolutely nothing to say to each other.'

'It's not Rick's conversation that turns *me* on, Bart,' she said smoothly.

He looked at her, his eyes puzzled. 'What do you mean?'

'Sleeping with a celebrity as famous as Rick, and knowing almost every other woman in the world would like to take your place, is a pretty powerful aphrodisiac.'

'That's a disgusting thing to say! Haven't you any respect for yourself?'

'Respect has nothing to do with sex—surely *you* know that. After all, you were willing to buy me, weren't you?' she retorted. 'That doesn't show much respect, does it?'

To her amazement a wave of red flooded his cheeks.

'I've already apologised for that,' he said abruptly.

'Not noticeably,' she said. 'But that's really beside the point. Saying sorry doesn't necessarily put things right.'

'Then perhaps this will,' he ground, and before she knew what was happening, he pulled her hard towards him.

The grip of his hands was tight, and though she tried to release herself from his hold, he would not let her go.

'Stop pretending, Melissa,' he said thickly. 'You've wanted this just as much as I have.'

His mouth clamped on hers like a vice, stifling her denial in her throat. Again she struggled to free herself, but his grasp tightened, his fingers digging into her bare flesh.

This was the first close physical contact they'd had, and as she fought against him she was conscious of his strength. It was like battling with a steel door. He moved his hand along her back to cup the nape of her neck, his fingers lightly caressing the soft skin at the nape. Then he lifted his mouth and moved along her cheek to the lobe of her ear.

The warmth of his breath was finally her undoing, and with a low murmur she clasped her arms around his head. She felt safe and comfortable in his hold, and knew a feeling of helplessness. Tentatively her lips touched his cheek. The skin was smooth and the intensely masculine scent of his aftershave assaulted her nostrils, tantalising her senses. She trailed her lips along his face, down the side of his jaw. Here the skin was rougher, and it stirred her in a way she had never experienced before. Languorous, erotic thoughts tumbled through her mind as she imagined him making love to her, exploring her, awakening her until she was lost to everything but her need of him. A weakness enveloped her and she trembled, clinging closer, exulting in the firmness of his hold, and the hardness between his thighs.

His head lowered and once again he covered her mouth with his own. This time his touch was tender, and he gently rubbed her lips. Strangely, he didn't go beyond this, a man in complete control of his desires. It was as if he'd proved his point, and for the moment that sufficed.

The intensity of her own response frightened

her, for she knew that if he had wanted to take
her now, she would not have resisted. What
was there about this man that could make her
disregard logic and sound reasoning? Why
hadn't she recoiled from him when she knew
his need for her had nothing to do with
affection? He would use her until he tired of
her, and then discard her like all his other
women.

Sickened by her thoughts, she found the
strength to push him away.

'You're despicable, and completely amoral.'
Melissa marvelled that she could speak with a
semblance of control, when only a short while
ago she had been totally devoid of it. 'I repeat
my request, Bart. Have this plane turned round
at once, and take me back to Los Angeles.'

He regarded her with self-assured calmness.
'If I hadn't known how much you enjoyed that
kiss, I would.'

'That was pure instinct,' she retorted. 'You're
an attractive man, and experienced. You know
how to arouse, and——'

'You wanted me,' he finished for her. 'I
could have made love to you any way I chose—
sitting, standing, lying on the floor, on the
couch . . .'

'That's a filthy rotten lie!' she cried. 'How
dare you even say it?'

'I dare because it's the truth,' he answered
unperturbed. 'And it's about time you admitted
it. The act's over, Melissa. Whatever you felt
for Rick is nothing compared to what you feel
for me.'

Her chin tilted. 'The only thing I feel for
you is contempt.'

'Perhaps. But I'm not concerned with your loftier emotions, only the basic ones.' His glance was sardonic. 'I've gone to a good deal of trouble to have you to myself for a few days, and I don't intend to be put off by denials.'

'What will you do if I refuse to give in to you—rape me?' she sneered.

'Would you like me to?' he asked softly.

Melissa's lips clamped firmly shut. Dear God! How was it possible to hate someone so much, yet want them to make love to you at the same time?

'I see you prefer not to answer the question.' Bart was speaking again. 'It was a pointless one anyway, because you won't refuse me when the time comes.' He touched her lightly on the arm. 'Come on, Melissa, let's have lunch and be friends again.'

She marvelled that he could switch his feelings on and off so easily. But then, she reminded herself, he was a man of considerable experience and, however much he wanted her, he would not be overwhelmed by his passion, as she had been.

'You're forcing me to accompany you against my will, and haven't even the decency at least to pretend it's because you want anything from me other than sex.' Her tone was derisive. 'And you want us to be *friends*?'

'You may look sweet sixteen, Melissa, and even act it at times, but, as we both know, you're not an innocent little virgin who needs lies to overcome childish scruples.' He was speaking calmly, and studying her reactions carefully. 'But there's no point in pretending I love you. You amuse and interest me,' he continued. 'And that's more than I can say for most women I've had affairs with.'

Melissa sighed wearily. 'It's pointless to continue arguing. Short of jumping out of the emergency exit and killing myself, there's no way I can get out of here—and even though the thought of going to bed with you sickens me, I don't regard it as a fate *worse* than death!'

He smiled. 'I'm glad that, in spite of everything, you've retained your sense of humour.'

She shrugged. 'With no money, and no credit cards, I may as well give in gracefully, and try to enjoy the next few days.'

'How about the nights?' he asked.

'I'll close my eyes and think of Rick.' Deliberately she lied with the intention to wound. 'That way, whatever happens, *you* won't enjoy them.'

His jaw clenched, but it was the only sign he gave of temper. 'Even if you *were* mad about him, I'd make you forget him.'

'Lover extraordinary, are you?' she jeered.

'I've had no complaints.' He refused to rise to the bait. 'When you want to stop pretending you don't want me, let me know, Melissa. Until then, I suggest we drop the subject.' He moved to the bell to summon the stewardess. 'How about cracking a bottle of champagne before we eat?' he said. 'Or do you feel in need of something stronger?'

When the Dom Perignon was wheeled in by a different hostess from the one who had first greeted them—there were three, Melissa found later, to attend to their needs—her first instinct was to crack the bottle over Bart's head. But though the thought gave her childish satisfaction, she recognised the foolishness of the impulse. Instead she settled back in her seat, if not to enjoy her favourite drink, at least temporarily to drown her sorrows in it.

CHAPTER SIX

WHEN they finally touched down at Nice Airport, the city was in virtual darkness. Not surprisingly, as it was three o'clock in the morning. But Customs were still very much alert, and stared curiously at them when they presented their passports with no luggage in evidence. In fluent French, Bart explained that the trip had been a whim, and that they intended to purchase clothes while they were here. Used to the foibles of the rich, the man gave a typically Gallic shrug, and waved them through.

A white, chauffeur-driven Mercedes was waiting for them outside, and headed along the Promenade des Anglais towards Cap Ferrat. Melissa lay back against the soft leather of the seat and shut her eyes. The movement of the car was soporific, the swish of the tyres a lullaby, and, exhausted after the long journey, she was soon fast asleep.

The crunch of wheels on gravel brought her back to consciousness and she opened her eyes, momentarily at a loss as to where she was. But as she felt Bart's hard, wide shoulder pressed against her own, so she remembered, and instantly moved away from him.

'Feeling better?' he asked solicitously.

'No—worse,' she answered grumpily.

'In that case, go straight to your room and sleep it out.'

Melissa made no reply, and looked out of the window. They were parked in front of an enormous two-storied villa, the lower floor painted pink, the upper slate-hung. Ultra-modern in design, it was floodlit.

'The view from the back is breathtaking,' Bart informed her as he helped her out. 'I envy your first sight of it.'

Although Bart had done his best to restore her good humour during the journey, Melissa's response still barely ranged on the civil.

'I have been to the Riviera before,' she said indifferently, 'and I'm quite familiar with the scenery.'

'OK, Miss Blasée,' he smiled good-humoredly at her rebuff, as he had done at several others during the last twelve hours.

The front door opened and a servant appeared. A warm welcome ensued in French, and Melissa was introduced.

'Jacques will show you to your room, and if you want anything to eat or drink, just ask him. You'll find most things, other than a nightdress, in your room. But, I'm afraid, if you wear one there's nothing I can do about it until the morning. The chauffeur will run you into Monte Carlo after breakfast,' Bart said.

'I'll need more than a nightdress,' she answered coolly. 'I can hardly manage with one dress and a bikini until we leave.'

'I realise that. Naturally I meant you can buy whatever else you want as well.'

'How about you?' She could not contain her

curiosity. 'I suppose you're in the same position.'

He shook his head. 'I keep a complete wardrobe down here, as I do in my other homes.'

'Wealth has its compensations,' she said drily.

'You make it sound as if it has drawbacks too.'

'It does—but I'm too tired to discuss them with you now.' Without bothering to say goodnight, Melissa crossed the white marble floor to the staircase.

Pine and wicker lent a deceptively simple air to her bedroom, and the small sitting-room adjoining. The walls were cream, as were the long-haired rugs on the floor, and pretty turquoise and cream striped cotton was used for both furnishing coverings and curtains, which fluttered lightly at the windows.

As Bart had said, virtually all Melissa's requirements were in her room, but she was too tired to sample any but the most basic and, after a quick shower, climbed into bed. There was something marvellously sensous about the feel of crisply laundered sheets against naked flesh, but she had little time to appreciate it, for within minutes of her head touching the pillows, she was asleep.

Hot sunlight flooding into her room awoke her, and she yawned and stretched lazily, enjoying the sound of the surf hitting the rocks below. How wonderfully refreshed she felt, and how, under different circumstances, she would be looking forward to the day ahead.

But the thought of Bart, and how he'd got her here, still niggled.

He'd certainly not exaggerated the panoramic sea-views though, and when she finally made her way downstairs at eleven o'clock, she was even ready to admit it grudgingly.

'Mr Huntingdon very much regrets that he couldn't wait to have breakfast with you, *mademoiselle*,' Jacques informed her, as she reached the hall. 'He had business to attend to, and won't be back until late this afternoon. Albert,' he named the chauffeur, 'will drive you into Monte Carlo as soon as you're ready.'

This was delivered in French, and Melissa assumed Bart had told the man that she too spoke it fluently.

'Where do I have breakfast?' she asked, deciding it would be indelicate to question Jacques as to whether Bart had mentioned how she was to pay for her purchases. Knowing how efficient he was, she was convinced arrangements had been made.

'On the terrace outside the living-room,' he said. 'If you'll kindly follow me . . .'

The vast room encompassed several separate seating areas, unified by an overall blue and white colour-scheme. Here, again, several wicker chairs added a pleasing touch of informality to the more streamlined look of the rest of the furniture. Sliding glass doors along one entire wall led out to the terrace and gardens, from where one had spectacular views seawards.

Seated in solitary splendour beneath a blue awning, at a white wrought-iron able that could have seated a dozen, Melissa sipped fresh orange juice before starting on the warm, buttery croissants and home-made apricot jam.

'They were delicious,' she complimented the manservant when, some fifteen minutes later, he came out again to enquire if she wanted anything more. 'As good as the ones I had at Mr Huntingdon's home in Los Angeles, and they're the best I've ever tasted.'

'Berthold will be very happy,' the Frenchman beamed. 'He's André's son, and there is a friendly rivalry between him and his father.'

As Melissa had suspected, there were no difficulties over payment for her clothes. Albert, the chauffeur, simply took her to the shops frequented by Bart's mother and two sisters, and whatever she bought was charged to their account. Naturally, there was nothing cheap in any of them, and though she disliked the idea of being beholden to Bart in any way—even though her predicament was of his making—she decided it was stupid to economise and buy less than she really needed, simply out of misbegotten pride. The choice was fairly limited though, as it was the end of the season, and it took longer than she'd originally anticipated to find what she wanted.

Although curious as to Bart's whereabouts, Melissa had not attempted to question the chauffeur. Discretion appeared to be part of his staff's training, and she passed the time on the drive back to the villa much as she had on the way *to* Monte Carlo—discussing the country's economy. Frenchmen loved to grumble, and this one was no exception: taxes, inflation, the uncaring attitude of the young. Albert had an absolute beanfeast!

It was nearly four o'clock when they drew up outside the front door, and Melissa hurried upstairs to change into a bikini. There were big decisions to be made too—where should she have her swim? In the magnificent kidney-shaped pool in the garden, or the sea, reached by steps cut in the rocks? Both glinted jewel-like in the sun, and looked equally tempting.

But her mind was made up for her when she came downstairs and found Bart waiting for her, also dressed for the water.

'Have a good day?' he enquired, eyeing her as if he were mentally undressing her, and clearly liking what he saw, if the sudden beating of the pulse in his throat was anything to go by.

'An expensive one,' she said. 'And you?'

'Tiring,' he answered. 'I'll tell you about it when we've had a swim. How do you fancy racing me to the raft?'

It was moored a short distance from the small, man-made beach, and with a shrug she accepted the challenge.

'It won't be much of a race, though,' she said. 'You're much faster than me.'

'In which case I'll give you a few yards' start.'

But even so he beat her and, teasingly triumphant, hauled her up to the wooden slats of the raft to sit beside him.

'It's obvious you're feeling better than you were the other day,' he commented, noticing that she was nowhere near as breathless.

'A little,' she admitted, as she squeezed the water from her hair.

'And towards me?' he smiled. 'Am I back in your good books again?'

'You can't be back somewhere you weren't in the first place!'

He shook his head. 'I never usually have so much difficulty making a woman admit she's wild about me!'

'Perhaps the type of women you're used to say what they know you want to hear!'

He gave a hearty chuckle, then pushed her back into the water. Although it took her by surprise, Melissa managed a deep breath before she went under, and to pay him back, swam beneath the raft and came up on the other side for another quick breath of air, before disappearing again. Moments later Bart dived in, and she swam beneath him, and grabbed hold of his legs.

'You little devil,' he said, as he dragged her to the surface. 'I thought you'd drowned!'

'Which would have meant a lot of wasted effort on your part,' she retaliated. 'Where would you find a replacement for me at such short notice!'

He smiled at her retort but made no answer. Instead he ducked her under again, then laughingly helped her back on to the raft.

For the next hour they swam and sunbathed; there was still plenty of warmth in the sun, despite the lateness of the hour. Afterwards they sat on loungers relaxing in the dying rays with champagne and peach juice, brought to them by Jacques.

Sipping her drink, Melissa stared out at the sea still dotted with boats and zig-zagging water skiers. A whisper of a breeze disturbed the red-gold tendrils of hair from her face as they dried, and the longer strands stirred against the floral cushions of her sun-bed. It was an idyllic way to while away time, and for some reason she felt more relaxed here than she had in California. Bart too seemed different, and more carefree.

She cast him a surreptitious look. He lay with eyes closed, but it was clear from his breathing he was not sound asleep. But she went on looking at him all the same, admiring the natural sheen of his skin. It was tanned almost mahogany, so that the silky mat of dark hair on his chest was barely noticeable. As if aware of her attention, he opened his lids, and sherry-brown eyes met aquamarine ones. She felt the blush rising to her cheeks at her being caught, and hoped he would mistake it for sunburn.

'Those few minutes were just what I needed.' He stretched lazily. 'Unlike you I didn't go to bed. I had some business papers to go through.'

'You'd better have an early night and catch up on your sleep.'

He smiled. 'I can manage on very little.'

'Cat-napping is a gift. I envy you being able to wake up feeling refreshed.'

'I'm gifted in others ways too,' he drawled. 'Care for a demonstration?'

His warm glance made his meaning obvious, and Melissa decided a change of subject might be a good thing.

'How much time do you spend here?'

'About five or six weeks a year—but not all at one time, of course,' he added.

'Where's your main home?'

'Pittsburgh,' he answered surprisingly. 'Do you know it?'

'Only that it's the steel capital of America, and that someone once said it was a wonderful place to leave!'

'That was true a while back,' he answered, accepting the quote in good part, 'but not today. It might not have the thrusting excitement of New York or even Chicago, but it's clean and modern and far from a backwood culturally. The Mellons and Huntingdons have seen to that.'

'Do you live with your family?'

'Good heavens, no.' There was amusement in his voice. 'I only use my parents' homes when it would be inconvenient not to—like Los Angeles. I don't have a place of my own there because it's a city I prefer not to visit unless I have to.'

'Does that apply to the whole of California?"

He shook his head. 'I love the coastline around San Francisco, and the city itself is one of my favourites.' He frowned. 'Mind you, as far as scenery goes, Pennylvania take some beating. Our hills and lakes are completely unspoiled, and very beautiful.'

'Are you sure that's not just home-state bias?' she teased.

'Not at all,' he answered emphatically. 'One day I hope you'll see it for yourself.'

'Going to kidnap me and take me there as well?' she responded flippantly.

'I won't need to.' He eyed her. 'You'll come with me because you want to.'

Idly, Melissa stirred her drink with a swizzel stick. 'You sound very sure.'

'I've never forced a woman to do anything against her will,' he said flatly. 'And that goes for you too. Whatever happens between us will be because we both want it, not just me.'

'That wasn't the impression I got on the way down here,' she replied carefully.

He sat up and swung round to face her. 'I'm afraid that was a joke that misfired,' he confessed. 'I was coming down here on business anyway, and I thought you might find it fun to tag along, as you didn't feel up to joining Rick. I was going to tell you the truth as soon as we were airborne, but when you started jumping to conclusions and getting angry, I decided to keep quiet and play along with it.'

Melissa could not prevent a grin, as much from relief as amusement. So she'd completely misjudged him, and if her usual sense of humour had come to the fore she needn't have wasted the past thirty-six hours treating him like a leper.

'You mean all that guff about wanting me was a lie too?' she asked, beneath lowered lids.

He leaned towards her. 'Of course not,' he said with quiet vehemence. 'But I didn't bring you down here to force myself on you. I just thought that away from Rick and his influence I might stand a chance of making you fall for *me*.'

'You've made me feel rather foolish,' Melissa admitted, 'but I guess my attitude had something to do with the fact you wouldn't let me leave the house when I wanted to.'

'I assure you I had no ulterior motive about that either,' he asserted with conviction. 'I genuinely didn't like the idea of you wandering around Los Angeles on your own.'

'Exactly what kind of business brought you here?' Melissa asked, with forced casualness.

But Bart wasn't fooled. 'Still don't believe me, eh?'

She shrugged. 'I have a suspicious nature.'

'There's no need to state the obvious!' he chuckled, and leaning across, placed his hands on either side of her chair. 'We took over some old perfume factories up at Grasse a few years back and turned them into a canning plant. We've been experiencing difficulties with the unions over production, and I came down to try and sort things out. If you still don't believe me, I'll take you up there tomorrow and you can check my story with the strikers.'

Melissa was completely convinced by his explanation, and no longer doubted that he was telling the truth. What reason would he have to lie anyway?

'I hope it won't be necessary, though, and that we can make a fresh start right away.' Bart was speaking again.

'Why not?' Melissa decided there was little point in further prevarications. She was here, so she might as well enjoy it as best she could. While she had no intention of falling into his arms, she would at least be pleasant. 'I must phone Rick and let him know where I am, though,' she said. 'He'll be worried.'

The wide mouth tightened. 'He knows you're here. I rang him last night to tell him.'

'He couldn't have been too happy about it,' she commented questioningly.

'Rick's happiness doesn't concern me.' Once

again Bart's eyes moved over her body, as though removing the two wisps of silk covering it, and this time she felt herself redden under the intensity of his gaze. 'I hope by the time we return, it won't concern *you* either,' he finished meaningfully.

More than ever Melissa longed to confess the truth about the charade, but once again her sense of duty prevailed. She would have to speak to Rick herself, and ask him to release her from their agreement. But what would happen if he refused? Wasn't it better to see how things developed between herself and Bart first—or rather, *if* they developed, she amended—instead of placing her employer in an unnecessarily invidious position?

'That depends on your powers of persuasion!' she joked.

'If you'll change into one of your new dresses, I'll take you to dinner and begin to cast my magic spell!'

'Smart or casual?' she asked.

'Which would you prefer?'

'Casual—or do you only know three-star restaurants?'

'Wouldn't you love it if I said yes?" His eyes crinkled attractively at the corners. 'Then you could accuse me of being a food snob.'

'Not at all,' she protested. 'It's just that when you're rich you're inclined to think the most expensive is always the best.'

'It's dangerous to generalise,' he warned. 'You should see people as individuals, not stereotypes.'

'Rich people tend to follow a particular pattern.'

He shrugged. 'Perhaps in Rick's circle—but not where old money's concerned.'

Melissa felt a sense of disquiet at his patronising tone. 'You may not be a food snob, Bart,' she snapped, 'but you *are* a snob.'

Thoughtfully he pinched his lower lip between forefinger and thumb. 'You're quite right,' he admitted after a few moments' consideration. 'Perhaps you can cure me of it.'

The sharp answer she was on the point of making died as she saw the seriousness of his gaze.

'I'll try,' she said.

'Good—and I'll try not to get annoyed when you correct me. It's refreshing, but takes getting used to.' He stood up. 'Turning back to the subject of food, will you trust me to book somewhere suitable, or would you prefer to recommend a restaurant?'

'And give you the chance to criticise *me*!' she smiled. 'Not likely.'

Pleasantly surprised that Bart had not only taken her criticism seriously, but accepted it without rancour, Melissa went up to change. It was strange that she'd ever though him austere and aloof. He had simply built a protective shell around himself to ward off predators who might be attracted to his money and the power it represented, rather than to the man himself. Realising it, she could excuse it.

The dress Melissa chose was simple in the extreme—though the price hadn't been! In pure white linen, it relied for its effect on the starkness against her tanned skin, and the moulding of the material to her body. It was impossible to wear anything beneath it, and this was obvious to anyone with half an eye. Definitely not *de rigueur* for a vicar's tea-party, but certainly a good choice to hold a man's attention!

She kept her make-up as simple as her hair, and after being washed and blow-dried, it fell in soft, silky waves to her shoulders. Wickedly innocent was the description that jumped to mind as she stood in front of the mirror for a final inspection—a cross between Mary Poppins and Alexis from *Dynasty*!

But her thoughts were very much in the latter vein as she came down the stairs, and Bart came from the lounge, whisky tumbler in hand. He exuded an air of tightly reined passion that added to his sensuality. It was a passion that was tempting to break down, and she wondered if any woman had ever succeeded completely.

He'd chosen a restaurant situated in the hills above Nice, which she knew well. One could dine either indoors or out, and because the evening was mild they decided to eat on the terrace overlooking the twinkling lights of the city. Gazing across at Bart as he studied the menu, Melissa felt like pinching herself to make sure being here with him wasn't just a dream.

'What are you going to have?' he enquired, looking up and catching her eyes upon him. '*I'm* not available until after coffee!'

'Mind reader!'

They chose their meal, and chatted about nothing in particular until their first course arrived. They'd both ordered one of the house specialities, soufflé of crab with lobster sauce, and Bart, who was the first to taste it, expressed his approval.

'Who brought you here?' he asked, when for the second time a waitress came over and greeted her by name. 'Rick?'

'I did have a life before him, you know!'

'You mean other boy-friends?'

'If you want to know if they were lovers as well, then the answer is no!' she said bluntly. 'Though why it should matter if I've had one or hundred, I really don't know.'

'Don't you?' he said flatly.

'Do I detect a note of disapproval?' she asked with genuine surprise.

'You don't strike me as the promiscuous type, that's all,' he prevaricated.

'Now who's putting people into pigeon-holes?' she countered.

'What's that supposed to mean?' he growled.

Melissa put down her spoon. 'You're not a fool, Bart. I'm sure you know exactly what I mean.'

'Okay, so I don't like to think you'd go to bed with any Tom, Dick or Harry who asks you,' he flung.

'Only Bart, I suppose.'

The wine arrived, and there was silence while it was poured.

'I——'

'You——'

They laughed, as they both started to talk at once, and silently Melissa pointed to Bart. 'You go first.'

'I was going to suggest we stop quarrelling and enjoy the meal.'

'Quarrelling won't stop me enjoying *my* food—in fact it adds a certain piquancy!'

He smiled. 'Wait until you reach my age. It will give you indigestion!'

'You don't seem old to me,' she asserted truthfully.

He looked at her in silence, then began to eat his soufflé again. 'I'm thirty-five,' he said suddenly. 'We're a generation apart.'

'Hardly,' she protested, 'and anyway, talk of age is ridiculous. It's enjoying being with someone that counts.'

'I suppose I think of you as being even younger than you are because you look like a teenager—even in *that* dress,' he added with a smile. 'You've the face of a child. That full mouth, the sweet, freckled nose, even the way your forehead curves: a baby face!'

'Well, I certainly don't see *you* as a father figure!' As so often happened, Melissa spoke her thoughts without thinking, and she debated whether to continue.

She wanted him more than any other man she'd ever met, and only Rick was standing in her way. But where did loyalty to Rick end and her own happiness begin? She was twenty-five, far too old never to have experienced a proper affair. She'd be a fool to turn down an opportunity like this, with no strings attached on either side. Yet hadn't she always professed to needing strings attached before giving herself to a man? Damn, damn, damn. Why was everything so confusing?

'What *do* you see me as, then?' Bart's enquiry cut short her reverie.

Melissa willed herself to raise her head and face him squarely.

'A lover,' she said boldly, not giving herself time for more thought, or to change her mind.

His head tilted, and the look he gave her was quizzical. 'I'm delighted, of course, but what's brought on this sudden change of heart?'

'Time . . . We've only a few days, and I don't want to waste any of it pretending.'

Silence was enforced on them—an obviously impatient one on Bart's part—as their plates were cleared and the entrée served.

'What happens when we get back to Los Angeles?' he asked, as soon as the waitress had left.

'Aren't you rather jumping the gun?' she evaded. 'I might turn out to be a disappointment, and you'll be glad to be rid of me.'

'I won't.' It was a flat statement.

She couldn't help smiling and, seeing it, his jaw tightened. 'You don't believe me, do you? That's why you're smiling.'

'On the contrary. I was amused at your certainty. You always manage to make you opinions sound unequivocal.'

'That's becuase they always *are*.'

'Modesty is not *thy* middle name!' Melissa laughed.

But Bart was not amused, and he reached across the table and took her hand in his.

'Contrary to what you think, it's not just sex I'm thinking of, Melissa—I want all of you, and for a long time to come.'

She would like to have asked him what a long time meant, but could not bring herself to do so. But she wasn't foolish enough to think he meant a permanent kind of relationship.

'Your meal's growing cold,' she said instead, and began to eat her liver.

'Does that mean you want to change the subject?' There was levity in his deeply timbred voice.

'Postpone,' she corrected lightly.

'That's good,' He gave an exaggerated sigh of relief. 'For a moment I thought *you* might have grown cold!'

He gave full concentration to his duck and, not wanting him to remark on her own lack of appetite, she made herself finish her meal. He saw her as a girl of experience, and there was no point in drawing attention to her attack of nerves.

She glanced at Bart from beneath lowered lids. Eyes half closed, he was sipping his wine. Savouring its aroma—perhaps even comparing the taste to his own brand. The thought suddenly occured to her that he would savour a woman in much the same way; understand her moods, encourage her when she needed it, absorb her into his system little by little, so that like vintage champagne he could appreciate her to the full. Yes, there was no doubt, he would be a dream lover.

Yet this still did not fully explain her capitulation, her weakened resolve, the discarding of a principle she had clung to for years. There was only one logical answer. Suddenly the glass of wine she had been about to put to her mouth slipped from her fingers, splashing not only the pink tablecloth, but the skirt of her dress as well.

'Don't worry,' she heard Bart say, as if through a thick fog. But she couldn't concentrate on what he said afterwards, and sat zombie-like as a waitress hurried over and attempted to dry her skirt with a serviette. *She was in love with Bart.* Yet how could she be, when until a few days ago, she'd disliked him thoroughly?' Or had she? Her dislike had been fanned by her loyalty to Rick, but she been attracted to him from the beginning. Thinking back on her inconsistent behaviour Melissa realised she'd half known it for some time, but hadn't wanted to face up to it, frightened of the implications. And she was still frightened of them.

'Worse things happen than a spilled glass of wine.'

Melissa blinked, as if coming out of a deep trance, and forced herself to answer, thankful that the accident could explain away her behaviour.

'But this dress was very expensive,' she cried. 'And I doubt if the stain will come out. If only it had been white wine instead of red.'

'Be thankful it wasn't hot black coffee, or we'd have had burns to contend with as well!'

'Don't be so damned nice about it,' she snapped, for some reason close to tears. 'Six hundred dollars is a fortune to pay for a dress, and it aggravates me to think I've probably ruined it first time on.'

'But you're not footing the bill, I am.' His tone was still placating. 'So if I don't mind, why should you?'

'But you *should* mind,' she argued tightly. 'Waste is despicable however much money you have, when there are millions of people starving in the world.'

'That six hundred dollars won't go very far divided between them!' he joshed.

'That's just the sort of answer I'd have expected from someone like you!' she blazed. 'You've never had to earn any money, so you haven't any respect for it—or at least not the right kind,' she amended.

He regarded her steadily. 'Are you deliberately trying to start an argument?'

'Of course not,' she denied hotly. 'I'm just trying to show you that I'm not impressed by your money.'

'Okay, so you've shown me,' he replied evenly. 'Now can we drop the subject of that blasted dress?'

Melissa guessed he was deliberately controlling his temper because he was anticipating making love to her, and didn't want to upset his chances by arguing with her. Irrationally, this goaded her on.

'I'd like to go home. I've a headache,' she announced abruptly.

'What a shame,' he said with concern. 'I'll get the check at once.'

'I'll wait for you in the car. I'm feeling chilly too.'

Before he could answer she stood up and headed for the car park. But when she reached the Mercedes she found it locked. Well, she couldn't go back after stalking off the way she had, so she'd just have to wait. He wouldn't be long. She glanced down at her watch. Eleven o'clock. A few minutes ticked by. For goodness' sake, how long did it take to settle a bill? Five more minutes passed, and still no sign of him. Melissa moved to the far side of the car park, so that she had a good view of their table without being seen. Bart was still there, leaning back in his chair, and smoking a large cigar. As she continued to watch, he was served with coffee and petits fours and as far as she could see there was no sign of a bill anywhere. Perhaps there was a query. No restaurant was infallible, and she remembered how carefully he'd examined the tab at Jimmy's when she'd lunched with him in Los Angeles. He had a typical rich man's mentality. Penny-wise, pound-foolish—or should it be cent-wise and dollar-foolish in his case? Whatever. He didn't mind leaving her standing in the car park for twenty minutes while he had the bill re-checked to save a few dollars, but he could shrug off six hundred as if it were nothing. But then common sense prevailed. He obviously didn't remember he'd locked the car, so he could hardly be blamed for not rushing.

But as he sauntered over some ten minutes later, his first words dispelled this illusion.

'Learned your lesson yet?' he drawled.

'You mean you knew the door was locked?' she rounded on him heatedly.

'Of course—it's something I do automatically.' Ever the gentleman, he opened her door first.

'Then why the hell didn't you tell me?'

'You didn't give me much of a chance, remember?'

Melissa banged it shut, and he went round to the other side, and climbed into the driving seat.

'You deliberately took your time, didn't you?' she accused.

He set the Mercedes in motion and backed out on the road. 'Yes,' he admitted, unabashed. 'You needed to be taught a lesson in manners.'

'I don't need lessons from you on how to behave, thank you,' she retorted.

'Perhaps a spanking might be more appropriate, considering how childish you were.' He took his eyes off the road for a moment to look at her. 'But I'm willing to accept an apology.'

'Well, I'm not willing to give one,' she answered defiantly. 'What are you going to do about it? Make me walk home?'

'I'd like to, but it's no safer for a woman to wander around Nice on her own than it is Los Angeles.'

'Your concern for me is touching,' she sneered.

'That's more than I can say for your snide comments. They're getting on my nerves.'

'You do have them, then?' she enquired witheringly. 'I was beginning to wonder.'

He shrugged. 'You seem determined to pick a quarrel—though for what reason I've no idea. But I'm equally determined not to argue with you.' He tried to stifle a yawn. 'Frankly, I'm too tired. I may not need much sleep, but forty-eight hours without, plus jet lag and you to contend with, is too much even for me.'

'Does that mean you're too tired to make love?' Now why had she said that? Couldn't she leave well alone, or at least give herself time to sort out what she really wanted?

'I'm never too tired for that,' he said matter-of-factly. 'I've just lost the desire as far as you're concerned.'

'Really?'

'Yes, really,' he reiterated patiently. 'Now why don't you close your eyes and take a nap. I think you're overtired too.'

'On the contrary. My headache's gone and I'm wide awake.'

'Then I suggest hot milk and a sleeping tablet before you go to bed.'

'Hardly a replacement for you,' she said contrarily. Damn him. Why should he be in control of his emotions when hers were so turbulent? 'I'm sure I could arouse your interest again quite easily.'

Melissa placed her hand inside his jacket, and began to undo the buttons of his shirt. But as her fingers on his bare chest began to arouse him, he jerked away from her, so suddenly that the car swerved, and had his reflexes not been so acute, they would have crashed into the wall on the far side of the road. As it was he braked so sharply that the Mercedes stalled.

'You little fool! What do you think you're playing at?' he demanded furiously, as he started up the engine again.

Colour stained her cheeks, but fortunately Bart was unaware of it. It had required every ounce of her willpower to touch him so intimately, to act so wantonly, and her consternation at his rejection was acute. Yet why had she done it in the first place? What was she trying to prove? That she had the power to arouse him? Any pretty girl could do that. The only explanation was that she wanted

him so much herself, she couldn't bear the
idea that he could take her or leave her.

'Cat got your tongue?' she heard him ask
witheringly.

'No—I just didn't think your question required an answer . . . that I needed to state
the obvious.'

'Nothing about you is obvious, Melissa,' he
snorted. 'One minute you say you want to go
to bed with me, the next you're freezing me
out, and then you change your mind again. For
God's sake decide what you really want.'

Melissa sighed. If only she could.

The port of Nice gave way to the Corniche,
and Bart changed into a lower gear for the
climb. Stars twinkled down from a cloudless
midnight-blue sky, and a full moon lit a
panorama of breathtaking splendour, illuminating the sea to dappled silver. In spite of the
twisting road, Bart kept up quite a speed, as if
he were putting all his hostility into his driving.
But there was no danger. He knew the road
well, and as it was near the end of the season,
there were few cars about.

'Has Rick asked you to marry him?' Bart
asked suddenly.

Surprised by the question, Melissa was
uncertain how to answer it. 'He's . . . he's
mentioned it, but I don't know how serious he
is,' she improvised. 'He talks about having
children.'

'Strange . . . He's never struck me as a man
who wants to perpetuate himself, or at least he
didn't when he was married to Jessica.'

Melissa had no desire to explore Rick's
relationship with his ex-wife. She was far more

interested in learning as much as she could about Bart, and what *he* wanted.

'How about you?' she asked. 'Do you feel the need to perpetuate yourself?'

He changed gear again, and his fingers lightly brushed against her leg. 'Of course,' he answered. 'I just haven't found a woman I want to perpetuate myself with.'

'You've had enough girl-friends.' Melissa was treading in deep water, but had gone too far to stop now. 'None of them good enough for you?'

'Not in the way *you* mean,' he answered smoothly. 'But certainly none of them had everything I want, and as I regard marriage as a commitment for life, I prefer to remain single until I find someone who does.'

'You sound as if you're looking for perfection.'

He shrugged, aware of the implied criticism. 'Unfortunately I haven't the nature to accept compromise.'

'Eighteen-year-old virgins are few and far between these days, Bart!'

He smiled. 'That's the last thing I want.'

'What's the first?'

'Someone who doesn't bore me,' he answered surprisingly. 'Like you, Melissa. You're the most mercurial girl I've ever met.'

Hesitantly she ran her tongue over her lower lip. 'Is that just a compliment, or a proposal?'

He chuckled. 'I'll answer that when I get to know you better. At the moment you only fill one of my requirements!'

Melissa turned her head away and stared out of the window at the pretty town of Beaulieu.

Sleeping with Bart had seemed so easy before she'd realised she loved him, but now she was scared it would bind her more completely to him, and make their parting more difficult when the time came. And part they would— sooner rather than later. What he'd just told her only confirmed that he saw her as little other than a pleasing interlude.

The car drew to a halt in the villa's driveway, and Bart came round the side to help her out.

'Well, is it yes or no?' he asked, looming tall above her.

'Hardly the most romantic of propositions,' Melissa commented drily.

'You've got the stars and the moonlight. What else do you want—a declaration of love?'

Because that was exactly what she did want, Melissa was hurt by his jokey tone.

'Let's leave it for tonight. shall we?' she said with deliberate casualness. 'As you so rightly said, we're both exhausted.'

She walked ahead of him into the hall, and was about to go upstairs when he caught her by the arm and swung her round to face him.

'Is that all you have to say?'

Her heart seemed to skip a beat, and then pounded furiously. Suddenly nervous of him, she fought to remain outwardly calm.

'What more do you want me to say? Thank you for a nice evening?'

'If it wasn't, it was entirely of your making,' he accused. 'You need help, Melissa. You've obviously got problems.'

'Really? What kind?' she asked with exaggerated innocence.

'Sexual—as if you didn't know.'

'Just because I changed my mind about going to bed with you?'

'No—because you're frightened to.'

He was right, but not for the reason he suspected. 'Don't be ridiculous,' she snapped.

His eyes were so near she could see them clearly in the zig-zag crystal light overhead, their sherry-gold flecks making them look like polished ingots.

'Then why not prove me wrong?' he said thickly.

'I'm no longer in the mood,' she answered coolly.

'I'm sure I can remedy that.'

In one swift move he was gripping her under the knees and swinging her up into his arms.

'This is what you really want, isn't it, to alleviate your conscience about Rick?' he said as, effortlessly, his long legs mounted the stairs two at a time.

'Put me down!' she cried, kicking her legs up and down in an effort to force him to loose his hold. 'This caveman act doesn't suit you!'

'I agree—but you gave me no choice. I'm tired of being given the runaround, and I don't intend to waste the whole of your stay *chasing* you, when you're more than happy to be caught!'

He kicked open the door to his bedroom, the noise echoing in the huge villa. Whatever must the servants think? Melissa wondered. But it was obvious Bart wasn't worried, for after dropping her unceremoniously on to the centre of his king-size bed, he slammed the door shut with equal force, then began to undo the buckle of his trousers.

'You haven't much on,' he said, as they dropped to the floor. 'But I suggest you remove it.'

The room was lit by a soft glow from the floodlit terrace outside, and Melissa could see Bart clearly. See too, as he rapidly stripped, that he was fully aroused, and that nothing was going to stop him making love to her now. Not that she wanted it to. In spite of her misgivings, now he'd forced her into this position, she'd no intention of fighting him further.

As he came towards her, her heart began to pound even faster.

'Don't tell me you're shy too?' he said, pulling her into a standing position, and adroitly unzipping her dress.

It slipped to the floor, and Melissa pushed it away with her foot. Uncertain if this was a sign of capitulation, Bart regarded her quizzically.

'Aren't you going to finish what you started?' she asked softly, and wound her arms around his neck, nuzzling against the thick grey hair that grew into the nape.

With a groan he pressed his lips savagely on hers. 'I want you, sweetheart,' he muttered against them, and ran his hands across her shoulders and down her back. 'God, how I want you!'

Gently he eased her lace panties over her slender hips, and then she was lying on the bed again, with Bart gazing down on her, his eyes making passionate love to firm, tip-tilted breasts, sweetly rounded stomach, soft, silky thighs, even before he tantalised them with mouth and tongue to a quivering response.

Lips parted, nipples hardened, hips arched,

she pressed herself against him, glorying in the feel of her flesh against his. Taut, firmly muscled flesh that responded to the questing of her hands, seeking to awaken, excite, to lose, to drown, until all was forgotten but pleasuring each other.

Melissa was lost: lost in a sea of passion, overcome by wave after wave of desire. Beneath his lips she moaned, moaned for the pleasure that was lifting her higher and higher, until she reached a crest of longing from which she begged release.

Teasingly he refused, allowing the peak to subside, though never allowing her senses to dull entirely.

'I love you,' she whispered, as momentarily he stilled to feast upon all of her with eyes clouded by desire. 'Oh, how I love you, Bart.'

'I'm crazy about you too, my darling,' he said huskily.

Then it was no holds barred, until they peaked together in violent, juddering, shattering waves.

Yet still they did not part, clinging together, their bodies warm and moist after the exertions of their passion.

'It was so good,' Bart murmured, as he rolled over on to his side, taking her with him. 'S-o-o very good, little one, I never wanted it to end.'

Melissa sighed contentedly, and nestled against Bart's chest, her cheek resting on the soft, curling hair. In spite of their intimacy, with their passion now spent, she was suddenly too shy to speak. Had he realised her innocence, or had his accomplished arousal, in which he'd made her lose all her inhibitions, hidden it from him? Certainly she'd felt very little pain. Had he guessed that what she felt for him was above desire, and that she loved him with all her heart and longed for him to reciprocate?

'I'll never get enough of you.' Bart's voice cut across her thoughts. His fingers too, as he softly traced the outline of her flushed cheeks, then moved along her swollen lips, to her chin, tilting it slightly so that he could kiss her. 'Never,' he reiterated against her mouth, and slowly began to rotate his hips.

The pleasure was agonisingly wonderful, lifting her to new, unbelieved heights, and when they finally climaxed again, it was a sensation altogether different from the first time: less animal, less draining, more sensual.

'Stay the night with me.' Bart kissed the tip of her nose, and lay back, eyes closed, against the pillows. 'Stay with me every night, darling, from now on,' he whispered drowsily.

'What will the servants think?' Melissa teased.

'They're French,' he smiled, and opened heavy-lidded eyes momentarily. 'They'd think it odd if you didn't!'

CHAPTER SEVEN

FOUR sun-filled days and four passion-filled nights followed, each different, and each equally exhilarating in its abandonment. Although Bart left the villa early for Grasse each morning, he returned to lunch with her—long, leisurely meals, during which they drank wine, swam and then made love on one of the terry-clothed divans in the lavishly appointed poolhouse. Afterwards he showered, changed, and then went back to the negotiating table with the unions, usually arriving back about six o'clock.

On their last evening, they decided not to eat at a restaurant, but to dine on the terrace, and Bart insisted that Melissa choose their meal.

'Ever since you told Berthold his croissants were as good as his father's he's been longing to prove that everything he cooks is.'

Because the chef originated from Marseilles, Melissa chose bouillabaisse for their first course. More often than not it was served as a main one, and as it was so filling, she decided to balance it with something light for the entfee— *Médaillons de Veau à l'Estragon* with a green salad. For dessert she plumped for strawberry tart—out of season, but apparently no problem— on a bed of crème patisserie.

Yet in spite of her happiness of the past few

days, changing for dinner that evening, Melissa felt depressed. Tomorrow morning they would be leaving, on her part probably never to return. That she loved Bart more than she would ever love anyone else she knew unquestioningly, and that he felt something for her more than mere sexual attraction she also knew. Not because of his murmured endearments during their sexual encounters—on his part 'I love you' was an illusory term, and one he had doubtless expressed to many women before her—but because later, when they were together, relaxed, all passion spent, he had enjoyed her as a friend. And what friends they had become, never tiring of their own company, never bored or needing the distraction of others to amuse. They had joked, laughed, discussed, quarrelled, and then made up, revelling in each reunion, both of mind and body, with equal enjoyment.

Would it all change when they returned to Los Angeles? she wondered. Was his interest in her a transitory thing, or did it have staying power? Before she saw Rick again, she hoped she'd know.

These questions were still uppermost in her mind later that evening, as she sat next to Bart on the terrace, sipping pink champagne, though to all outward appearances she was completely carefree.

'You look more beautiful than ever tonight.' Bart's gaze was warm as he raised his glass in a toast to her.

'It must be love,' she answered lightly.

'In that case you should return the compliment,' he smiled and reaching across, drew her hand to his lips, holding it there for a moment before running his tongue gently along the tips of her fingers.

She gave a small shiver at the contact. 'OK,' she smiled back. 'You look more handsome than ever tonight.'

But Melissa was no more convinced than before. It was the moonlight talking, not Bart. She needed proof that he loved her, not words. She sighed inwardly, and turned her eyes to the sea, as smooth as a mill-pond, and reflecting shards of silver on the water.

'Why so quiet?' he asked.

'I was having romantic thoughts,' she improvised hastily.

'Care to share them?'

'Why not?' she smiled. 'I was thinking that if you had a yacht we could sail away into the sunset.'

'Won't flying off into it do?'

'Too mean to buy me a yacht?' she teased.

'I'd buy you the world if you wanted it, Melissa,' he said huskily.

'Don't tempt me. I might take up that offer!'

'In that case we'll go shopping first thing in the morning!'

Melissa laughed. 'Are you always so accommodating to your girl friends?'

'Of course.' He slanted his eyes at her. 'Though so far you've been comparatively cheap. Hothouse strawberries for tonight's dessert won't exactly leave a hole in my pocket!'

'You've forgotten about the clothes,' she said. 'Or haven't you had the bill for them yet?'

He shook his head. 'Those were necessities, not gifts.'

'Are you sorry to be going back?'

'Very—because it means that Rick will come between us again unless you've already made up your mind which of us you want.'

If only she could tell him there was no choice to be made, but to a degree, she still felt honour-bound to Rick. He telephoned every day, and at first she'd been surprised at his total lack of curiosity regarding her relationship with Bart. It could not be entirely explained away as his being too occupied with his own affairs to care. But then she'd discovered Bart had told Rick that his reason for taking her with him to France was a dread she'd developed of staying on in Los Angeles after her attack.

'He said you were still nowhere near well enough to join me, and I must say it was very thoughtful—at least it stopped you flying home.'

'Flying home?' she'd echoed questioningly.

'Yes—I gather you wanted to return to London. Thank heavens you didn't, Melissa. It would have really put the cat among the pigeons.'

Rick had gone on to say that the movie was going well, and that he'd discovered Jessica had a suitor—a French count, who was also an astute and respected banker of considerable means.

'She's not in love with him, of course, but gossip has it that she fancies the idea of being a countess. It will be one up, at least, on all her social register pals! She needs a little push, though, to make up her mind, and I'm planning on giving it to her.'

Because Bart had been waiting impatiently for her to rejoin him, Melissa hadn't bothered to enquire what Rick had meant by a 'little push', and it only came into her thoughts now because she wondered if perhaps that was what Bart needed to propose, for she suspected he was in love with her, and that like herself until a few days ago, didn't realise it.

'Have you decided, Melissa?' Bart's voice repeating his previous question brought her sharply back to the present.

'Not yet. I——'

Her answer was cut short by the appearance of Jacques, to announce that dinner was ready, and she was relieved when the subject was not reopened.

'Do you prefer to stick with champagne, or go on to wine?' Bart asked, as they seated themselves at the candle-lit table.

'I'm easy—but then you know that already!' She smiled.

'In other words you'd rather stick to champagne!' He requested another bottle of Roederer '26, and Jacques disappeared to fetch it.

'No expense spared tonight, I see,' Melissa teased.

'I thought you might have tired of the ten-franc plonk from the local supermarché!' he grinned.

'I bet you've never even tasted it,' Melissa said.

'Once, and once only,' he admitted. 'And that was only to compare it to the Californian equivalent.'

'You mean your own?' she enquired sweetly.

He chuckled. 'I promised to take you round our vineyards, didn't I?'

She nodded. 'But I won't hold you to it. I know how busy you are.'

'I can always make time for you,' he said

seriously. 'In fact, it might not be a bad idea to fly straight there instead of returning to Los Angeles. How do you feel about it?'

'I'd like that very much.' If it meant prolonging the time they were alone together, she'd agree to fly to the moon with him.

'We'll have to land at San Francisco—there's nowhere nearer that can handle the 707,' he told her. 'But I can easily arrange transport down to Napa from there. It's only a hundred and twenty-five miles or so, and we could drive it in a couple of hours, or use the helicopter if you prefer.'

The champagne arrived along with the bouillabaisse, and Melissa declared the fish soup the most delicious she'd ever eaten.

'It has that wonderful fresh sea taste,' she declared.

'Not surprising, considering the fish was alive until just before Berthold placed it in the kettle,' Bart said drily.

She made a face. 'You're putting me off.'

'It's no different from oysters,' Bart smiled. 'They're practically still discussing the latest price of pearls as they slip down your throat!'

'That's one of the reasons I've never tasted one,' she said.

'What are the others?'

'They're grey and slimy-looking.'

'Amazing, isn't it, that something that looks so unappealing can be one of the most delicious foods in the world—they're pretty good for the libido as well,' he added with a sly grin.

'You must be eating them secretly!'

'What's *your* excuse?' he flashed back.

Melissa laughed, and reached across to touch

his hand. 'I do love you, you know,' she said softly.

'So you've told me once or twice,' he answered solemnly. 'But whoever said repetition's boring is a damned liar!'

Melissa dabbed at her mouth with her serviette, and leaned back in her chair, replete for the moment.

'Are you always different when you're down here?' she asked

He looked surprised. 'I wasn't aware that I am,' he said. 'Care to tell me in what way?'

'Every way.' Melissa shrugged and took a deep breath. 'Your sense of humour is sharper, you act younger, you're less opinionated, less reserved, more——'

'Hey, hang on there. You're making me sound like a Jekyll and Hyde! Am I really such a boor back home?' he asked in mock horror.

'A boor—but never a bore!' she smiled.

His lips curved appreciatievly at the pun. 'If what you say is true—and I don't doubt you, golden girl—then I can only think you've wreaked the change. No-one's ever teased me the way you have—or for that matter, given me as good as I've given them.'

'Not even your family?'

He gave her a sardonic look. 'I'm the youngest child, and an only son—does that answer your question?'

'All God's gifts,' she commented wryly.

When the meal ended, and coffee was served, Bart asked Melissa if she'd care to dance.

'It'll be a change to hold you in my arms vertically!' he joked.

'Getting bored with the other way?'

'Mmm. You'll have to think up something new to re-awaken my interest!'

It was strange how much she enjoyed exchanging sexual banter with Bart, when previously it had bored her. But then everything connected with this man was enjoyable and interesting, and made every other pale into insignificance. The slightest touch, the brush of his hand on hers, could arouse, and often she'd been frightened at the intensity of her response. It was difficult to be in the same room without touching him, feeling the urge to hold him, kiss him, make love. Away from him he filled her thoughts, with him she knew peace of mind.

Bart danced with relaxed ease, using his body with the same dexterity of movement as a pianist gliding his fingers over the keyboards, and Melissa gave herself up to the pleasure of the rhythm: her skirt swirled around her, and her hair fanned out across his broad shoulder as her cheek rested against his, excited, as always by the touch of his skin. She raised her eyes slowly and saw his springy grey hair above the collar of his blue silk shirt. He was a conservative dresser, a man completely without fripperies, and his clothes—even sports ones—though impeccably cut, were restrained both in style and colour. The only jewellery he wore was a gold and steel Bulgari watch; no signet ring, no gold chains, no bracelets.

'Why so silent?' he asked, as the tape changed, and the vibrant voice of Carly Simon began to sing 'Nobody Does it Better'.

'I don't like talking when I'm dancing,' she answered truthfully. 'Why strain your voice to be heard above the music when there's no need?'

'But there is,' he insisted. 'I like having sweet nothings whispered in my ear!'

As if to illustrate his point he drew her even closer, but now the steps Bart did bore no relation to the tempo, and were merely sinuous movements of his body, making her conscious of his thigh against hers, and the hard strength of his chest as it pressed against her breasts.

'How about going upstairs and letting me prove that "Nobody Does It Better"?' he whispered, some time later, as the tape ended. 'I want you so much, sweetheart.'

Melissa had no need to reply. He was aware of her answer in the trembling of her limbs, the dampness of her skin, the panting gasp she gave as he placed his mouth over hers. Desire scorched through her like a flame, and when they reached the bedroom, they could not get their clothes off quickly enough. She ached with the need to be taken by him, to be filled with his velvet hardness.

'Don't make me wait,' she said huskily, as his hands moved sensuously over her body. 'I'm ready for you now.'

He plunged into her with a ferocity she had never known, and she groaned with pleasure, exciting him further with the movement of her hips as she encouraged him to thrust deeper and deeper, faster and faster, until they exploded in a climax that was bone-shattering in its length and intensity.

'That was beautiful,' he said thickly, gathering her to him and kissing her gently on the lips. 'I never tire of you, Melissa. Each time we make love I think it can't get any better, and then it does.'

'It's the same for me, darling,' she answered softly. 'That's why I can't bear the thought of leaving here.'

'Don't worry. I guarantee the same satisfaction in the States!' he said thickly.

Melissa smiled and caressed his skin with her fingers. 'It won't be the same, though,' she said. 'There are pressures there we've not had to think about.'

'You mean Rick?' Bart's tone, as always when any reference was made to the actor, grew cooler, much, *much* cooler, and he reached out to turn on the bedside lamp, flooding the room not only with light, but with a certain harsh reality.

'No—I was thinking more of us and how you see *our* relationship,' Melissa answered as casually as she could. Perhaps the time was now right to force Bart into some kind of admission of intent. She plumped up the pillows behind her, and sat up, drawing the sheet around her at the same time. She didn't want him distracted in any way until he had cleared up some of her uncertainties. She wanted a future with him, and he'd intimated that was possible. She had to know for certain what kind he envisaged.

But he remained silent, and it was a few minutes before he replied. 'I see us being together, which means, of course, giving up your job . . . leaving Rick, that is, and coming to live with me.'

'You mean be your mistress?'

He smiled indulgently. 'For a modern miss you use some mightly old-fashioned words,' he said.

'Don't patronise me, Bart,' Melissa snapped.

'The word may be *passé,* but can you think of a better one to describe a kept woman?'

'I'd be quite happy for you to go on working, if that will make you happy,' he drawled. 'I'm sure I could find you a good spot with one of our companies. You're a smart girl, Melissa—too damn smart to be just a secretary.'

'Thanks—but when I want to change my job, I'll find one for myself.'

'Well, you certainly can't go on working for Rick—or were you thinking it might be fun to play us off against each other? Say six months in the States, and six months in London, perhaps?'

Melissa studied Bart's face for some sign that he didn't mean what he'd said, and that perhaps he was testing her in some way. But he was too much in control of himself to give anything away. Suddenly he'd changed, and was as aloof and restrained as when she'd first met him.

'That's a rotten thing to say,' she flared. 'Surely you know me better than that by now?'

He shrugged. 'I want you, angel—and that means accepting you as you are.'

'How big of you,' she said sarcastically.

He shifted slighty beneath the sheet, and laid a hand placatingly across her hunched knees.

'What I really mean is that I don't want to share you. I want you to forget Rick and concentrate on me.'

Melissa forced herself to look directly at him. 'With a view to what?'

'Not marriage,' he answered flatly.'

His blunt rejection seared through her like a red-hot poker, and it took every ounce of her acting ability to keep it from showing.

'I'm not surprised. You've managed to avoid

it for thirty-five years, Bart, and I didn't imagine a penniless nobody like me would stand a chance of succeeding where daughters on the social register have failed.'

She waited for him to argue that her status had nothing to do with their relationship, but he didn't even have the decency to pretend.

'I knew you'd understand, that's why I haven't tried to lie to you. I respect you too much to make plans or promises I've no intention of keeping.'

So much for her hopes that he'd fallen in love with her. What a fool she'd been ever to imagine his feelings ran thet deep. He wanted her physically, enjoyed talking to her, respected her opinions, enjoyed her humour, yet in his book, this didn't add up to love. She still had the vital ingredients of social position and money missing. The knowledge hurt desperately—to care for someone as deeply as she cared for Bart, and be aware his regard for her would never be enough to make her his wife, was almost more than she could bear. She had to give him up now. It would be hard to say goodbye, but in three months, six months, perhaps even a year, when he grew tired of her, or even worse, decided to marry someone else, it would tear her apart.

But she must not tell him yet. He might take it as a sign of provocation, and try to dissuade her, and she was not sure she had the strength to hold out for long against any blandishments. Once back in San Francisco she could phone Rick, and ask him to book her a flight back to London. He'd have to take his chances with Jessica from now on. Whatever happened, she could no longer live under the same roof as Bart.

'No lies ... no regrets. I guess that *is* the best way, Bart,' Melissa said equably.

The look on his face was unmistakable, and she guessed he'd not been expecting such as easy victory. She smiled bitterly to herself. Within twenty-four hours he'd learn he'd been right not to.

'We'll make plans on the flight back,' he said across her thoughts.

'What time are we leaving?'

'Late afternoon. The unions are ready to sign a new contract, and I'll be driving up to Grasse in the morning to complete the negotiations.' He half turned away to reach for the light switch, giving Melissa a view of his profile: the thick grey hair waving straight back from the high forehead, the firm, straight line of his nose, and the narrow but well-shaped mouth. Why couldn't he love her? Why? Why? Why?

'Meanwhile the night's still young,' Bart went on huskily, and reached for her. 'Don't let's waste any more of it talking.'

But though Melissa responded immediately to his touch, he seemed to sense her change of mood, and made love to her gently, sweetly, comfortingly, before finally losing himself in his own burgeoning desire.

Later, when he'd fallen asleep, she returned to her own room, the only time she'd done so since the first night they'd made love. But it had been impossible to lie impassively by his side, the touch and smell of him still lingering on her body, reminding her of the passion they'd shared, and would never share again. For on his part it had been a passion without emotion, a mindless coming together like copulating animals, not an interweaving of soul and heart.

Love was a stranger to Bart, and might always remain so, as long as suspicion and insularity closed his mind to it.

CHAPTER EIGHT

THE flight back to San Francisco was as bad as Melissa had anticipated. Bad in the sense that she had to keep up a pretence while Bart talked of the future. She picked at her food, and refused all offers of drink, except black coffee, using the age-old excuse of a sick headache. She obviously looked sufficiently wan to convince him—after a sleepless night, who wouldn't?— and eventually he suggested she went into the adjoining bedroom and lay down.

'We've plenty of time to discuss things,' he told her, as she got on the bed.

'Yes,' she agreed. 'Plenty of time, Bart.'

'Weren't you feeling well in the night either, sweetheart?' he asked with concern.

'No—that's why I moved into my own room,' she lied.

'I missed you,' he said huskily. 'I never realised how wonderful it was to wake up beside a woman until I met you.'

Melissa felt a sudden stab of jealousy for all the women in his past, and for all the ones in his future. To hide it she closed her eyes, feigning a weariness she did not feel. She was far too tense, het up emotionally, dreading their arrival and the scene she guessed would ensue when she walked out on him. Bart was not the type of

man to take a rebuff easily—perhaps because it
was an unknown experience. Like everything
else in his life, conquests had come easily, and
he was the one who always did the turning
down.

She heard the door close quietly behind him,
and breathed a sigh of relief. She'd stay here for
the remainder of the journey, even though
her thoughts were bad company. However
troublesome, they were infinitely less disturbing
than Bart's presence.

The 707 touched down at noon, and with only
hand luggage they quickly cleared Customs. But
that was the last peace Melissa was to know for
some time. As they came into the main Arrivals
Hall a cluster of reporters and photographers
greeted them, and flashlights half blinded her as
they began to pop.

'What are you going to wear for the wedding,
Melissa?'

'Has he bought you a ring yet?'

'If you pushed it forward by a few hours you
could do a double act with Rick's ex!'

'How did you manage to hook him?'

The questions were thrown thick and fast, but
before Melissa could ask what they were talking
about—obviously there'd been some kind of mix-
up—she heard the unmistakable voice of Rick
calling her name.

'Darling, there you are! How super you look.
That little rest did you the world of good.' He
pushed through the throng, now made even
larger by a contingent of fans who had recognised
him, and caught her in his arms, kissing her
resoundingly on the lips. 'Just keep smiling and
let me do all the talking,' he murmured through

clenched teeth. 'I know this is a shock for you, but I'm afraid one of the crew leaked the announcement before I had a chance to warn you.'

'What the hell's going on?' Bart demanded, looking from Melissa to Rick, his face like thunder.

'I proposed to Melissa when I phoned last night, and she accepted,' Rick answered immediately. 'I made her promise not to tell you, and being the loyal girl she is, I see she kept her word.'

'Is this true?' asked Bart, his voice a mixture of disgust and fury.

'I—I——'

'Of course it's true.' Rick placed a protective arm around Melissa's shoulders. 'Now if you don't mind, Bart, old chap, we have to talk to the press. If you'd rather not wait, we'll both be happy to see you later on. We're spending the night at Stanford Court. Why not join us there for dinner? Meanwhile, many thanks for taking such good care of Melissa. She looks great.' He turned away and, holding up his hand, addressed the reporters as they clustered around and began to throw questions at random. 'OK, boys, one at a time, *please*,' he requested. 'My fiancée's exhausted, as you can see, and I'm going to speak for her.'

Bart strode off without a word or a backward glance, the hunch of his shoulders speaking volumes. But, trapped as she was, there was nothing Melissa could do about it for the moment, perhaps nothing she wanted to do about it. It certainly solved the problem of telling him she'd no intention of continuing *their* affair.

With half an ear she listened to Rick's lies, as he explained how they'd fallen in love, and the reason she'd gone to the South of France with Bart Huntingdon.

'As you may or may not all know, Melissa was mugged and badly beaten up during her stay in Los Angeles,' he told them. 'Our host, and wonderful friend, who's also the backer of my new film, *Gambler's Choice*, kindly offered her the facilities of his villa—until she could face returning to the States. As you can see, my proposal finally gave her the courage she needed.'

There was a good deal more show-biz schmaltz in similar vein, and with the adroitness of a professional, Rick handled even the most personal enquiries with panache.

'Whew, thank God that's over,' he said with relief, some half-hour later, leaning back in his chauffeur-driven Cadillac as it set off for the city.

'Now perhaps you'll tell me what the hell you mean by making an announcement like that without my permission first,' Melissa rounded on him furiously, all her pent-up emotions coming to the fore.

'Calm down, sweetie, calm down,' the star placated. 'I wouldn't have done it if it hadn't been absolutely necessary.'

'Absolutely necessary?' Melissa snarled. 'In my book that only covers life and death.'

'Exactly,' he answered smoothly. 'And death to Jessica's alimony puts new life in my bank account!'

Melissa sighed exasperatedly. 'And what's that supposed to mean?'

'Darling Jessica's getting married again,' he announced triumphantly. 'The count turned up in Vegas yesterday morning and gave her a final ultimatum. One of the extras happened to overhear it, and mentioned it to me. That's when I decided to announce our marriage plans first. I knew it would give her the final push she needed to accept,' he explained. 'In typical Jessica fashion she decided to go one better, which is just what I'd hoped and prayed for. They're getting hitched tonight at Caesar's Palace.'

'I see.'

'I knew you would.' Rick squeezed her hand. 'If you'd had a regular boy-friend—someone you cared for, I mean—I'd never have done it. But as things are . . .' He shrugged. 'Well, you'll just get a bigger bonus than usual at Christmas for being such a good sport—and a pretty good actress too,' he added with a grin. 'You really had Jessica fooled.'

Everything had happened so quickly, it was not until she was in her suite at the hotel that Melissa began to sort out her thoughts. Whatever Rick had said to the contrary, she doubted if anything would have stopped him announcing their marriage. Saving half a million dollars a year alimony meant far more to him than consideration for *her* feelings—or anyone else's for that matter—and if things had been different between herself and Bart, this final lie could well have put an end to their relationship. As it happened it was in tatters anyway. But that was not really the point. Rick was no fool, and whatever excuse Bart had given for taking her with him to France, he must have guessed there was more to it than consideration for her health. Yet without bothering to enquire first, he'd gone ahead with the announcement just the same.

Because of this she felt her loyalty to Rick was at an end, and even though it wouldn't change anything between Bart and herself now, if she ever saw him again she would tell him the whole truth and set the record straight. At least he'd know she was not the gold-digger he assumed her to be. But if his fury at the airport was anything to go by, he would have already left San Francisco, and she doubted if she would ever see or hear from him again.

But in this Melissa was wrong. She was in the bath when she heard a loud knock at the door of the suite and, grabbing a nearby towelling robe, she hurried, dripping on the carpet, to answer it.

Peering through the glass spy-hole, she was amazed to see the man uppermost in her thoughts standing outside in the corridor. Quickly she unlatched the safety chain and let him in.

He was still in a fine temper. It was apparent in the set of his shoulders and mouth, and the virulent look he gave her, so different from the ones she recalled during the past few days.

'I didn't expect to see you again,' she greeted him.

'The same goes for me,' he answered grimly. 'But I don't like being played for a fool by a cheap little tramp, and I want an explanation.'

'Hardly cheap, considering the company I keep,' she retorted, immediately on the defensive. 'And as for being a tramp—living with *you*

would have made me that! Marrying Rick makes
an honest woman of me—or is that expression
too old-fashioned for you as well?' she added
sarcastically.

He ignored the barb. 'You don't know the
meaning of the word "honest",' he grated.
'You've lied and cheated from the start!'

Melissa felt herself redden. Had Bart guessed
the truth all along? 'What—what do you mean?'
she stammered.

'Pretending that you cared for me, that I
meant something special to you, that you *loved*
me. And all the time you intended to marry
Rick.' He reached out and caught her by the
shoulder. 'But that wasn't enough for you, was
it?' You thought you might be able to do even
better for yourself, and get me to ask you to
marry you as well.'

'That's not true,' Melissa cried. 'You're not
making sense.'

'I'm making plenty of sense.' Dark eyes
stabbed at her. 'All that questioning last night.
Do you think I didn't realise the point of it?'

'I wanted to know where I stood with you!
Was that so wrong?'

'Yes—because it wasn't for the right reasons.
You're a rotten, evil, grasping bitch! I made the
mistake of believing you were more than you
appeared, but in fact you're just another tramp.
More high-toned and polished on the outside
perhaps, but inside you're dross!' He flung her
away from him, the gesture so violent she fell
against the wall.

A sharp pain shot through her shoulder, but
she ignored it. Compared to the pain in her
heart at this moment, it was as nothing.

'There was never anything between Rick and myself—it was all an act. An act to convince Jessica he'd never go back to her because he'd fallen in love with *me*.'

'And you were willing to go as far as marriage to help him out?' Bart spat out the words as if he wanted to hit her with each one of them. 'Have another try, Melissa. I wasn't born yesterday.'

'Of course I'm not going to marry Rick,' she denied impatiently.

'It didn't sound like that a couple of minutes ago, or have you already forgotten boasting he was going to make an honest woman of you?' Bart asked scathingly.

'I just said that to annoy you. I didn't expect you to start calling me names without giving me a chance to explain first.'

'In other words it was a lie?'

'If you like, but——'

'But nothing,' he interrupted curtly. 'You're incapable of telling the truth, Melissa.'

'That's not so,' she cried. 'I *am* Rick's secretary and nothing else. He was scared of Jessica's influence over him, scared he wasn't strong enough to resist her, and that she'd get him back unless he could convince her he was in love with someone else. I felt sorry for him, and when he asked me to help him out, I agreed.'

Bart's shrug made it obvious he didn't believe her, and she bit her lip. The sunlight pouring in from the sitting-room haloed his head and outlined his shoulders, making him look taller and broader. But with a pang she noticed how pale he was beneath his tan. In spite of what he thought of *her*, she still loved him as much as ever.

'You're a very well-dressed secretary,' he grated. 'That Geoffrey Beene alone cost six thousand dollars.'

'That was all part of the act to convince Jessica. Of course Rick paid for my clothes. I couldn't possibly have afforded them myself.'

'And was the mink coat also part of the act?' he asked witheringly. 'Was that also an absolute essential?'

'I bought it myself. It was a special offer and I got it cheap.'

'Now I know you're lying. Both of them were charged to Rick's account—I was with you when he phoned to tell you he'd taken care of them after they were stolen, and asked you to go in and replace them.'

Melissa felt the colour draining from her face. Damn, she'd quite forgotten. On such a slender thread she'd probably hanged herself.

'Trying to get out of that one as well?' she heard Bart jeer. 'Or are you finally stumped for an answer.'

'I'd forgotten my credit cards and my cheque book. Rick had an account at the store, and as they wouldn't keep it for me, I charged it,' she whispered, near to breaking point. 'I'd intended to tell him, but what with one thing and another I never got round to it,' she finished, well aware her story didn't have the ring of conviction, even though it was absolutely true.

'For God's sake stop the pretence!' He shouted the words and then with a great effort drew a deep breath. 'One of the things I liked most about you was your honesty, your willingness to call a spade a spade,' he said quietly. 'Don't spoil even that memory by acting the innocent. At least have the courage to admit the truth.'

'I have done,' she reiterated. 'Please believe me.'

'Would you believe me if I told you I'd just sprouted wings?'

'Try horns and I might!' she snapped back.

He flung her a look of disgust. 'That's a joke! I may not be a saint, but if anyone's a devil it's you, Melissa. A devil with the face of an angel!'

'Stop it!' She pummelled his chest with her fists with such force that he staggered back. 'You've no right to talk to me like that. I may have been foolish, but whatever I did wasn't meant maliciously. I only wish I'd told you about Rick and myself that first night in France when I realised I was in love with you—but unfortunately wishing won't change things.'

'*In love with me!*' Bart exploded. 'Obviously there are two kinds of love, Melissa, and yours has a different meaning from mine.'

He turned to walk out and she ran across to him, still hoping against hope that she could salvage something from the wreck, and she clutched at him to prevent him going.

'Ask Rick,' she pleaded in a cracked voice. 'He'll confirm everything I've told you.'

'I wouldn't believe anything that man said if God himself was asking the questions!' Bart wrenched her hands off him. 'Goodbye, Melissa. I wish I could say I've enjoyed knowing you, but other than in the Biblical sense, it's been anything but a pleasurable experience!'

Before she could answer he'd gone. She remained in the room as if rooted to the floor.

Nothing had changed, and yet everything had changed. In her heart of hearts she'd hoped that somehow, sometime, they'd meet again, and things would be different between them. He'd have missed her, realised she meant something to him, that he loved her. But now she knew it had been a foolish, desperate dream. Whatever they'd had between them was over before he'd even entered the room. His mind had been closed to her entreaties from the beginning, and the only reason he'd come here had been to give vent to his hatred.

Slowly she walked back to the bathroom. She must leave Rick, that was certain. Not just because of what he'd done—in all fairness, whatever he might have guessed, he hadn't known she was in *love* with Bart—but because he would be a constant reminder of him. She must go right away, somewhere where she could think about the future and get herself together again.

But where? There was only one place she knew that was perfect. Craigmar, her uncles' island.

By the time she met Rick in the bar for pre-dinner drinks, Melissa was completely composed. There were no sign of the tears that had racked her slender body, no sign of the blotched skin and red eyes. Skilful make-up could repair everything but a broken heart.

'I'm leaving you, Rick,' she announced over her brandy. She'd decided she needed something stronger than wine to give her a lift. 'As soon as Jessica's married, I'm flying home.'

'But why?' He looked at her aghast. 'I can't manage without you!'

'You managed before,' she said unsympathetically. 'There's no shortage of competent secretaries.'

He looked at her curiously, his handsome features for once intent on someone else's problems other than his own.

'Did you and Bart have something going between you?'

'A very little something—on his part, at least,' she couldn't help adding bitterly.

'So I didn't wreck anything then?'

'Let's say you didn't exactly help, either.'

'I'm sorry, Melissa, I just didn't think. But then that's been the story of my life,' Rick said apologetically, and placed a hand over hers. 'Is there anything I can do to rectify things?'

Melissa shook her head. 'It was more or less dead before we arrived back at San Francisco— you just nailed the lid on the coffin!'

'Care to tell me about it—it often helps to talk things out, you know?'

Melissa put down her drink. Perhaps a sympathetic ear was just what she needed. 'I'd like to do that.'

Leaving out the more intimate details, she recounted the whole tale, how Bart had engineered her on to the plane, and what had followed, concluding with their final row.

'He's a fool,' Rick growled as she finished. 'What does he want? Can't he recognise class when he sees it?'

'Only when it comes with a capital C!' Melissa answered drily.

'I warned you, didn't I?' Rick said. 'On the plane coming over I told you he was a son of a bitch.'

'You can't choose who to fall in love with, unfortunately.'

'You'll get over him,' the actor blithely assured her. 'Young hearts mend quickly.'

'Perhaps.' She sighed. 'But mine's never been broken before, so I wouldn't know.'

Rick gulped the last of his whisky. 'Now the ice has been broken with Bart, you could take up *my* offer instead of leaving. We might even make that marriage for real. A wife/secretary would be convenient to have around.'

Melissa smiled. Hardly the most romantic of proposals, but Rick was nothing if not practical!

'I don't think so, but thanks all the same,' she said.

'What do you intend doing?' he asked.

'I haven't made up my mind. I've enjoyed working for you, and I know I'll never again find such a glamorous job.'

'So don't give it up!' He saw her shake her head and he smiled ruefully. 'When are you returning to England?'

'As soon as I've collected my things from Bart's house.'

'Do I rate a goodbye kiss?'

'Of course.'

Lightly, she kissed him, and a moment later Rick disappeared to his own suite.

Turning to the news channel as she entered her bedroom, Melissa caught a bulletin which had just started, and Jessica's wedding to the Comte de Cherney was the headline.

At least somebody got her man, Melissa thought ruefully, and perhaps it was even one she really wanted!

She managed to get on a seven-thirty plane

to Los Angeles, and a connecting flight to Heathrow. It was a rush, but worth it. There was no sign of Bart at the house, and she didn't enquire where he was or if he was expected.

By the time she finally arrived at London Airport, Melissa was feeling completely disorientated from lack of sleep, and when she arrived at the flat she didn't even trouble to unpack before heading for bed.

When she eventually awoke it was light, and her radio alarm clock registered twelve-thirty, but it was not until she heard Katy's voice softly enquiring if she was awake that she learned what day it was, and discovered she'd slept for twenty-four hours!

'I had quite a fright when I saw your cases in the hall,' her friend said. 'And I've been dying to know why you're back so soon, particularly after the news of your engagment to Rick. But you looked so exhausted, I didn't dare wake you.'

Over breakfast, Melissa confided the story once again of her affair with Bart, and its disastrous ending.

'Why on earth did you allow him to believe you were penniless?' the other girl asked at the conclusion. 'If he'd known the last thing you were interested in was his money, things might have been different.'

'The fact that it affected his feelings for me was enough to make me realise he could never love me the way I loved him,' Melissa answered. 'Love has to be based on trust.'

'Anyone that rich is entitled to be suspicious,'

her friend argued. 'I would have thought you of all people could understand that.'

'My circumstances are different,' Melissa shrugged. 'Perhaps in that respect I've been lucky, I don't know. But what I do know is that if I loved someone and wanted him, his background or lack of money wouldn't stop me marrying him.' She swallowed hard. 'After the things Bart said to me at the hotel, it's pretty obvious that whatever he felt for me was superficial anyway. He didn't even believe me when I told him the truth.'

'Hardly surprising in the circumstances, particularly after that *faux pas* about the fur coat!'

Melissa put her face in her hands. 'The whole thing's a rotten mess,' she said unhappily.

'When Bart finds out you're not marrying Rick he might come after you.' Katy touched Melissa's arm consolingly.

'But only to ask me to live with him,' Melissa answered bitterly. 'And that's a proposal I'll never be interested in!'

The finality in her voice terminated the conversation, and Katy, as Rick had done only forty-eight hours ago, enquired what she intended to do now.

'I'm going to stay with my uncles—and I don't want anyone to know where I am. And I mean *anyone*,' she reiterated, fixing her friend with an intent stare. 'I have to have time to get myself together.'

'Okay,' Katy agreed. 'But what about your uncles? You haven't spoken to them for years. They might not be too happy to have you come and stay with them.'

'I'll keep well out of their way, so they'll hardly know I'm there,' she answered. 'Anyway, I don't intend telling them I'm coming. I'll simply turn up.'

CHAPTER NINE

CRAIGMAR, her uncles' island, was little more than a huge pile of rocks, where gulls circled and other species of birds nested and squabbled for every available nook and cranny. It was an ornithologist's dream, and Melissa could well understand her uncles' desire to live here. But that was where the dream ended, for nothing else about the bleak island was enticing from a human point of view. The wind blew continually, and often the seas that crashed incessantly against the rocks were so high that one could be marooned here for weeks on end. And yet it still had a beauty; a bleak beauty perhaps, but one that suited Melissa's mood of the moment.

'I'll come up to the house with you,' Willie MacIntyre offered. He was the local fisherman and also delivered household supplies to the island. 'Usually I leave the packages here, and Mrs Kylie collects them. But just in case you decide you want to come back with me . . .'

'That's sweet of you, but I think it's better if you go. Then my uncles can't send me back even if they want to—or at least not until you call next week!'

He looked as if he were about to argue, but then thought better of it. 'There's a telephone here if you decide you need me sooner,' he told her. 'It was only installed a couple of years back, and your uncles paid privately to have it linked up with the mainland. Something to do with keeping a check on their stocks and shares.' He smiled ruefully. 'They may be a wee bit eccentric, but not where making money's concerned!'

With a friendly wave, Melissa began the ascent, treading warily on the slippery steps, hewn out of the rock, which led to the vast Victorian slate-roofed edifice her uncles called home.

Planted squarely in the centre of the island, the granite building looked like something from a Hammer horror movie, and Count Dracula himself might well have found its twenty-odd rooms a comfortable haven.

Melissa recalled how frightened she'd been when she had first seen the house as a small child. Even to an adult it was slightly scary, and she wondered if she had been foolhardy to come here, and ignore all the warnings.

'Hullo, Mrs Kylie,' she said, as the oak front door opened to reveal a gaunt, angular-featured woman in her mid-sixties. 'I'm Melissa, do you remember me?'

'I've not gone senile,' she snapped. 'Of course I remember you. Wouldn't have recognised you, mind—except for the hair, of course. Not that you've grown much. You were always a wee thing.'

Not the warmest of greetings, Melissa reflected, but at least she hadn't banged the door in her face!

'What brings you here?' the grey-haired woman was speaking again.

'If you'll let me in, I'll be happy to explain. The breeze isn't exactly balmy!'

The door inched open, and Melissa eased herself and her case into the hall.

Nothing had changed, just faded. Flagged stone floors, grey stone walls, and massively ugly iron wall-brackets illuminating an exquisite and priceless collection of paintings and tapestries. Museum-like, the house was run at a constant temperature to protect the art treasures and a generator had been installed many years ago for this purpose.

At least I won't freeze, Melissa thought, as Mrs Kylie took her up the uncarpeted oak staircase, and showed her into the room she'd occupied as a child.

'I'll light the fire and put bed-linen on when I've time,' the housekeeper told Melissa. 'I'll tell your uncles you're here, but I doubt they'll see you before supper. That's served at seven—and don't be late.'

'I wouldn't dare,' Melissa smiled, but there was no answering response from the pinch-faced woman.

The door banged behind her and Melissa was alone.

Comfortably furnished, and painted in white—with no dust and no pollution, the room looked as if it had been decorated yesterday, but probably hadn't been touched for ten years or more—it was carpeted in warm rose, and contained a hand-carved four-poster bed. It had originally been used by her parents on their occasional forays to the island, and her mother had had a hand in the appointments. A bathroom

adjoined—another of her mother's innovations—
and though not luxurious, was perfectly adequate.

A gong rang promptly at seven, and Melissa
made her way to the dining-room. Her uncles
were teetotal, and wasted no time on pre-meal
fripperies, even when they had guests.

They were already seated when she appeared,
but when she hesitated in the doorway, uncertain
of their welcome, they beckoned her forward.

'Come in, come in,' Charles said testily. 'We
won't bite.'

She did as she was told, and sat down in the
chair he had indicated at the far end of the
table. Identical twins, at one time they had been
impossible to tell apart, except that Charles
always wore a gold and ruby signet ring, while
Robert did not. But time and illness had wreaked
havoc with Robert's looks. Thin to the point of
emaciation, and with very little hair, his skin
was parchment-coloured, where before it had
had the same pink-cheeked glow as his brother's.

'I've not been too well,' Robert told her, as if
reading her thoughts. 'Something to do with my
digestion.'

'Have you seen a doctor?' Melissa enquired.

'Don't believe in them. The Lord helps those
who help themselves, and I'm putting my trust
in Him.'

Melissa wasn't sure exactly what he meant,
and looked towards Charles for an explanation.
But none was forthcoming, and they went on
talking to each other, continuing the conversation
her entry had interrupted. It was conducted
almost in a whisper, and Melissa found it
impossible to follow. Instead she concentrated
on the pictures lining the walls—Turners and

Constables—enjoying them as much as when she had first seen them.

Even when Mrs Kylie entered with the soup they did not look up at her, drinking theirs noisily, like a pair of children. They had always been eccentric, but at least there had been some semblance of normality to their behaviour. Now there was none. They acted as if they had seen her a few hours ago, and showed no curiosity as to why she was here, how long she was staying, or what she'd been doing for the past ten years.

'I hope you don't mind my coming here,' she said at last, tired of her own company. 'I haven't been well, and——'

'Stay as long as you like.' Robert waved a bony hand in her direction. 'Just keep out of our way, though. Little girls should be seen and not heard—always remember that.'

She was about to say that she was no longer a little girl—true, she hadn't bothered with make-up tonight, and wore a plain skirt and twin-set, whose bottle-green colour was not dissimilar to a school uniform—but there was no way they could have forgotten her age. Only Mrs Kylie's hand on her shoulder, squeezing it hard, prevented her from answering, and the woman shook her head, indicating Melissa to keep silent.

'Come and see me in the kitchen afterwards,' she whispered, as she placed the meat course in front of her. 'It's no good arguing with them—other than for business matters they live entirely in the past, you see.'

Fortunately her uncles were quick eaters, and they'd left the table in under half an hour, nodding in her direction as they departed, but not bothering to say goodnight.

'How about a cup of coffee?' Mrs Kylie invited, when Melissa took up her invitation and joined her in the kitchen, where a cheerful fire burned in the old-fashioned range, and a fat, black cat curled sleepily in front of it.

'I'd love one.' She gave a friendly smile, and this time it was reciprocated.

'I must apologise for my behaviour earlier on,' the housekeeper said, as she filled the cups. 'I'm not used to visitors, and your uncles rarely talk to me now, other than about household matters, so I'm afraid I've forgotten even the basic social niceties.'

'Why on earth do you stay here?' Melissa asked curiously.

'I've no other home,' the woman answered simply. 'My family are all dead, and living here all these years, I've no friends. So where would I go?'

'You could get another job?' Melissa suggested.

'At my age?' Thin, veined hands fluttered. 'I'm getting on for seventy, Melissa, and on the island I more or less do as I please.

Although Melissa had never particularly liked the housekeeper as a child, she could not help feeling a sneaking sympathy with her now.

'You'll have me for company, for a little while at least,' she told her. 'I've had an unhappy love affair, and I wanted to go some place where no one would find me.'

'Your uncles won't mind how long you stay,' Mrs Kylie shrugged, expressing no curiosity to hear more. 'It's strangers they hate, and only themselves they love. If one ever goes, so will the other.'

Melissa shivered, in spite of the warmth from

the flames. 'Uncle Robert looks very ill,' she ventured.

'Cancer—with all the articles about it in the newspapers, you don't need to be a doctor to recognise the symptoms,' the woman answered.

'Can't you persuade him to go to the mainland and see a doctor?'

'*Me* persuade him?' The housekeeper gave a short, mirthless laugh. 'The only one he's ever listened to has been Mr Charles, and he's as dead set against doctors as Mr Robert.' She touched her head with the tip of her forefinger. 'They've some kind of religious mania—strange, really, considering they were atheists all their young years.'

'Perhaps they've developed some kind of guilt complex about it,' Melissa suggested.

But the woman wasn't interested in exploring the whys and wherefores of her employers' peculiarities. 'I'm off to bed now,' she said, rising. 'I never stay up later than nine.'

Thank heavens I brought my own radio with me, Melissa thought, as she went upstairs to her room. With no television, and no one to talk to, the evenings were going to be very long.

Strangely, this didn't turn out to be true. After clambering over rocks all day, often taking a picnic lunch, she was so exhausted from battling with the elements that she was ready for sleep by early evening. She saw little of her uncles other than at meal times, and Mrs Kylie told her that they were cataloguing their collection of English landscape artists.

'They must be worth millions,' Melissa remarked.

'What else did they ever have to spend their

money on?' the housekeeper sniffed. 'If you ask me, it's a poor substitute for wives and family, though.'

Melissa noticed a bitterness in the woman's voice, and wondered if she might have been in love with one, or even both of the brothers, when she was younger. But she was not the type you questioned on intimate matters, and Melissa delved no further.

The telephone was a godsend, for at least Melissa was able to keep in touch with Katy and hear what was happening to her, as well as gossip about their friends. It stopped her feeling completely cut off from civilisation.

'Everyone's asking where you are,' Katy told her. 'And dying with curiosity to know what happened between you and Rick. One day you're engaged to him, and a week later it's all off!'

'Well, they'll have to die for a while longer, I'm afraid. I'm still not ready to come back home.'

'Incidentally, they're not the only ones curious as to your whereabouts,' her friend went on. 'A private detective called Ross has been round here a few times, chatting me up and trying to wheedle information out of me. He's something to do with Bart, I gather.'

'I suppose he's read about the break-up too, and wants to see me again,' she answered.

'I think it's something like that, but Mr Ross is a close-mouthed type, and doesn't give much away.'

'Well, don't you either,' Melissa instructed. 'I've no intention of seeing Bart again, and I just want to forget he ever happened.'

Not that she could. He occupied her thoughts day and night, and she often wondered if she would ever get over him.

Melissa had been on the island six weeks when she finally decided the time had come for her to leave. She could not keep running away from the future, or from Bart. If his intention was to see her, then let him. She'd soon make it clear they could not pick up the pieces and start over again.

'Melissa, Melissa!' There was a loud pounding on her door, and she opened her eyes blearily. What time was it? Six-thirty, and still dark.

'Come in, Mrs Kylie,' she called. 'The door's not locked.'

'It's your uncles.' The woman was terribly agitated. 'They're not here. I've searched all over the house and they're not here,' she repeated.

'Perhaps they've gone for a walk.'

'At this time of the morning, and in this weather? It's pouring with rain!'

'What made you look for them at this hour?' Melissa asked curiously.

'I always get up at six and take them porridge and tea. But their room was empty.' Obviously close to tears, she clutched Melissa's shoulder. 'I've been frightened of this since Mr Robert fell ill.'

'You mean . . . you mean they may have killed themselves?' Melissa said slowly.

The housekeeper nodded. '*Please* get dressed and help me look for them.'

Hurriedly Melissa donned trousers and a thick, polo-necked sweater then, with Mrs

Kylie at her side, began a search of the island. But there was no sign of them.

'I wonder if they took the boat,' Mrs Kylie said suddenly.

'What boat?' Melissa questioned. 'I didn't know there was one.'

'It's not sea-worthy any more, and it's kept in a cave near the jetty; that's why you haven't seen it.'

They took the steps as quickly as it was safe, and the empty cave told them all they needed to know. In the turbulent seas the small craft wouldn't last a quarter of an hour. Robert and Charles had chosen to die as they had lived— together.

By the afternoon a police helicopter and doctor had been landed on one of the few flat plateaux of the rocky island, and it was not long before the two bodies were discovered floating in the sea a couple of miles off-shore.

'Obviously suicide,' the doctor said briefly. 'No need for a post-mortem. We'll fly the bodies back to the mainland and leave you to make the funeral arrangements, Miss Abbot.' He paused. 'Will you be coming back with us?'

Melissa nodded. 'I'd like to, if you'll wait while I throw a few things together.'

Melissa felt no sadness at her uncles' passing, and it would have been hypocritical to pretend otherwise. The funeral arrangements were soon made and she was surprised at the large attendance. It appeared that in spite of their many eccentricities, they'd been charitable men, particularly towards the local community. It was clear that while they'd not earned love and affection, they *had* earned respect and gratitude, and these were epitaphs to be proud of.

'Miss Abbot?' A plump, sandy-haired man stopped Melissa as she was about to enter the funeral car to return to the hotel. She immediately recognised Hamish Maguire, her uncles' solicitor, and her own too, until a few years ago.

He murmured a few words of condolence, and then told her he'd like to speak to her at the hotel.

'Of course. Why not ride back with me?' she offered.

With a grateful smile he accepted, but it was not until they were in the privacy of her bedroom that he told her she was the main beneficiary of her uncles' will.

'They left a goodly sum to Mrs Kylie—enough to keep her in comfortable circumstances for the rest of her life,' he said. 'But as for the rest—and it's many millions, my dear—you're the sole heir.'

'I assumed most of it would go to charity.' she answered in surprise. 'I've more than sufficient from my parents, and I really don't want any more.'

'What a pleasant sentiment,' the solicitor said respectfully, though it was obviously one he didn't share.

'It's not just that, Mr Maguire,' she said. 'I don't feel I'm entitled to it. It's like receiving a gift from strangers, and that's what my uncles were to me. I'd like you to draw up a list of Scottish charities—after all, this was their home—and I'll decide how the money should be distributed.'

The man looked aghast. 'I think you should at least sleep on it before you make a final decision,' he said.

'I won't change my mind,' she answered firmly. 'Though for the moment I don't want anyone to know about it. We'll dispose of the art collection first, and see what the final figure is.'

It did not take long for the national newspapers to get hold of the story. Eccentric multi-millionaires made wonderful copy, and reporters were soon swarming all over the island. Mrs Kylie, who had had little opportunity to speak for years, soon couldn't stop, and revelled in being the centre of attention.

Melissa, as the heiress, came in for her share of publicity too, and she soon became a target for begging letters and crank business propositions.

'Just burn them,' she instructed Katy, who'd taken a couple of weeks off work to stay with Melissa while Sotheby's valued and photographed all the paintings for the auction, to be held in the early spring.

There was a sound of a helicopter above the house, and Melissa glanced out of the window. 'I wonder who that is,' she said.

'Probably more reporters,' her friend answered. 'This is the best story since Howard Hughes died, and they're going to milk it dry!'

'Be a dear and see, will you—and if possible keep them away from me?' Melissa pleaded. 'I really feel I've had enough.'

Katy threw her a sympathetic look. 'You've stood up to it marvellously, darling, considering . . .' She hesitated.

'Considering everything that happened before,' Melissa finished for her. 'About the only good thing that's come from my uncles' deaths—apart from the people who will benefit by it—is the fact I've hardly had any time to think of Bart—or at least I've managed to cut it down to once or twice a day!'

Katy disappeared, and Melissa settled back once again to study the list of charities Mr Maguire had drawn up for her. Trying to decide which were the most deserving causes was not an easy task.

'Hello, Melissa.'

With a start, she dropped the pen she'd been holding, and heard it fall to the floor. The voice was Bart's.

She had been half expecting to see him, though not until she returned to London, and now the moment had come she was petrified. For several moments she remained motionless, her mind in a whirl. It was impossible to be rational when she was near him. In that respect, nothing had changed.

'Come to congratulate me?' she said finally.

'I tried to find you long before I knew you were an heiress,' he said quietly.

He seemed even taller than she remembered, but that was because he was thinner and had deep shadows beneath his eyes.

'So Katy told me,' she said coldly.

'So you did know.' He clenched his jaw as though trying to control the muscles of his face.

She shrugged. 'I didn't think we had anything more to say to each other. You made it obvious what you thought of me in San Francisco and I took that as final.'

'I was angry then . . . angry and hurt. I didn't mean most of what I said.'

'Are you here to enlighten me on the parts you did mean?' she questioned.

'I deserve your sarcasm, your contempt,' he said heavily. 'I behaved abominably.' He placed his hands on the desk and leaned towards her. 'Can you forgive me?'

'Why not? I don't need your money now, so I've no need to pretend I'm in love with you.'

He reeled back as if she'd slapped him across the face. 'You don't mean that, Melissa.'

'I don't say things I don't mean,' she said calmly, intent on hurting him as he'd hurt her. 'With all my money I'm going to make a new life for myself. Become part of the jet set— perhaps even marry into the aristocracy,' she added for his benefit. 'I guess I'm even good enough for a Huntingdon now. It's a pity you're the only one available.'

His skin went ruddy, emphasising the greyness of his hair, and she was suddenly aware of how white it had become about the temples. 'So I've wasted my time?' he asked huskily 'I thought . . . I hoped . . .'

'That at the sight of you I'd fall into your arms?' she finished for him, forcing a laugh. 'That's over, Bart. Whatever I felt for you, you killed when you told me I wasn't good enough to marry you. And then when you accused me of deceiving you, believed that I'd lied about loving you . . .'

'I told you I didn't know what I was saying! I was jealous . . . furious about your marriage announcement, and I wanted to hurt you as you'd hurt me,' he reiterated heavily.

'Furious because you're used to getting what you want, not because you loved me,' she flung.

'That's not true. I did love you . . . do love you . . . more than anyone or anything in the world.'

'Then why didn't you tell me . . . Why didn't you ask me to marry you?'

'Because I was a fool,' he said bitterly.

'And now you're no longer one,' she said witheringly. 'Now you've realised my worth— all ten million pounds of it!'

'Don't mock me, Melissa,' he pleaded. 'I made a mistake and I've paid for it. These past weeks have been agony.'

'Such agony that it's taken you a fortnight to get here. The news about me broke at the beginning of the month, Bart.'

'I was in the Australian outback—we've a sheep ranch there. I didn't hear about you until I got back to Sydney, then I flew here straight away.' He sighed heavily. 'There's not a day, not an hour I haven't thought of you, wanted you. Please, darling, say you forgive me.'

His expression was one of such pleading that she couldn't look at him without pain. Yet because she loved him so much, forgiving him was even more difficult.

'That last afternoon,' he went on, 'I'd made up my mind to marry you.' He saw her look of disbelief, and he flung out his hands in a gesture of frustration. 'It's true, Melissa, I swear it. Even though I believed you to be a girl with no morals, and that you were playing me off against Rick. I wanted you so much, I knew I had to have you as my wife. I didn't care about your background. I didn't even care if you didn't genuinely love me. I was so sure of how *I* felt, I thought it would be enough to make you come to love me in time.'

'Saint Bartholomew!' she jeered.

'No, just a man in love.'

'You had plenty of opportunity to tell me before we landed,' she said. 'Why didn't you?'

'Pride. When it finally came to it, I couldn't humble myself and admit you'd won,' he said raggedly, ignoring the scorn in her voice. 'If we'd gone on to Napa things might have been different, but when we arrived at the airport . . . well, I was glad I hadn't acted like a fool. Please, Melissa.' He came round the side of the desk and stood over her. 'Please——'

A knock on the door interrupted him.

'Come in,' Melissa called.

It was Katy. 'I'm terribly sorry,' she apologised, 'but I've held off as long as I could. It's Mr Farley,' she named one of the men from Sotheby's. 'He wants to speak to you. A query about one of the Constables.'

'I'll wait,' Bart said, and his tone implied he'd wait for ever if need be.

'I've never seen anyone look as wretched as that poor man,' her friend said, accompanying Melissa across the hall. 'What have you been saying to him?'

'Just giving him no hope.' Melissa shrugged, adopting an indifference she was far from feeling.

But the other girl knew her too well to be

deceived. 'You don't look much better yourself,'
she vouchsafed. 'Why go on being obstinate
when you're crazy about the guy? Put the past
behind you, and concentrate on the future.'

'Ever thought of writing an agony column!'
smiled Melissa.

'If you take my advice, I might think about
it!' Katy placed an arm affectionately around
Melissa's waist. 'Will you?'

'I don't know . . . I keep thinking, if only
he'd asked me before he found out about the
money from my uncles. He says he was going
to on the plane flying back to San Francisco,
but I don't believe him.'

'Why should he lie to you?'

'Because he wants me, and he's clever enough
to know it's what I want to hear.'

Her friend sighed. 'Well, I can't force you—
but I know what I'd do.' She stopped outside
the door of the dining-room. 'By the way, Mrs
Jeffrey's redirected a pile of mail here.' She
named the daily help at their London flat. 'I've
gone through most of it, and apart from the
usual begging letters and bills, there's a letter
from that detective Bart sent looking for you.'
She held it out. 'I recognised his name on the
back of the envelope, so I haven't opened it.'

'It can't be very important, but I suppose I'd
better read it,' Melissa said.

Mr Farley's query was soon dealt with, and
Melissa went back into the hall again and
stared at the envelope Katy had given her.
Slowly she tore it open. There was another
envelope inside and a single sheet of paper.

'I'm sure by the time this reaches you, Mr
Huntingdon will have already seen you,' the

detective had written. 'After all the publicity regarding your uncles, it's probable the whole world knows where to find you now! But just in case, I feel I should forward you the letter he instructed me to give you had I discovered your whereabouts earlier. He was most explicit that you and only you should read it.

'In conclusion, may I add that I've worked for the Huntingdon Corporation for many years, but never before has Mr Huntingdon concerned himself personally with any matter as he has this one. This may or may not be of interest to you. My guess is that it will be!'

It was signed 'Harvey Ross', and although Melissa had never met the man, from the tone of his letter she guessed she'd like him if she ever did.

With trembling fingers she ripped open the envelope containing Bart's letter.

'When I left you at Stanford Court,' it began without preamble, 'I knew it wouldn't be easy to put you out of my life, but I never expected it to be impossible, and that I wouldn't be able to carry on without sharing it with you. But each day that's passed, I've realised how much I'm missing by being alone—very much alone, golden girl, for without you I'm nothing.

'If I'd been thinking clearly, I'd have realised immediately you were telling me the truth about your relationship with Rick, but I was so full of jealousy, I couldn't think straight. You see, I'd made up my mind to marry you myself, and I'd intended asking you on the plane. But I had last-minute doubts again, and when you weren't feeling well, it provided me with a perfect excuse for postponing it. Then of course we arrived in San Francisco, and I was greeted with the announcement of your forthcoming marriage to Rick. Try and put yourself in my place, sweetheart, and imagine my feelings. The knowledge that you were going to be another man's wife blinded me to all reason.

'Call me proud, arrogant, selfish; I'm all those things and more, and the fact that you love me in spite of it makes me very humble. And you do love me, my darling, don't you? You're not the type to flit from man to man—I realised that the first night you slept with me. You were far from the girl of experience you pretended to be, and that made our union all the more satisfying, not less so. I never lied to you when I told you each time was more wonderful than the last, and since you there's been no one else. How could there be? You gave me the greatest gift a man could ever want, and I failed to recognise it—the gift of love.

'I tried to call you on the telephone to tell you all this, but you'd already left London, and your daily help told me you'd gone away too, and she'd no idea when you'd be coming back. That was when I decided to put Harvey Ross on your trail. I love you with all my heart, darling. Without you, life will have no meaning.'

It was signed simply 'Bart', and dated three weeks after she'd left San Francisco. The envelope too was franked with the same date.

As Melissa realised the implication of this, her eyes filled with tears of happiness. Bart had wanted her as his wife while he still believed she was penniless. He'd not been lying to her.

Determined not to waste another moment away from him, she ran back to the study. But when she reached the door, her hands were shaking so hard she couldn't turn the handle, and she had to clench them momentarily and dig her nails into the palms to stop them. She tried again, and this time she was able to open it.

Bart did not appear to notice her entry. He was staring out of the window, his thoughts far away. Wherever he was, though, it was not in some Elysian field, for the expression on his face was one of deep anguish.

Not taking her eyes from him, Melissa clicked the door firmly shut. As she had expected, the sound startled him, and brought him back to the present.

'Everything all right?' he enquired.

'Yes.'

'You don't look as if it is.'

'Only because I'm trying to pluck up the courage to apologise,' she answered steadily.

'What for?'

'For being a fool not to believe you.'

Not waiting to explain further, she ran over to him and put her arms around him, pressing herself close to his body. She felt him shudder, but he gave no other sign of emotion.

'I want to marry you, Bart——'

'What made you change your mind?' Still he remained leaden, and she stepped back and looked into his face, reading the uncertainty there. He was frightened to give full vent to his feelings until he was certain she meant what she said.

'The letter you wrote me. My daily help forwarded it, and I just read it. No woman could ever feel more wanted, Bart, and one day I'm going to show it to our children.'

He didn't answer at once, as if he still couldn't believe what he was hearing. 'I should never have left you in the first place,' he said heavily. 'If I'd listened to my heart instead of my head, I would never have let you go.'

'It didn't take you long to come to your senses,' she replied softly. 'The date on your letter proves that.'

'But I made us both suffer for nothing.' His voice was grim. 'I can't forgive myself for that.' With a groan he pulled her close. His fingers wound themselves around the silky, red-gold tresses of her hair, and he pressed tiny kisses on her eyes and the corners of her mouth. 'I love you so much, my darling, words can't express it,' he murmured. 'We'll never be parted again.'

'That's one thing I'm very sure of,' she said tenderly. 'Now don't talk any more, Bart, just kiss me.'

His lips were gentle and warm, growing less gentle as the fierceness of her response aroused him, telling him how much she wanted him.

Bodies close, they rested against each other. Melissa felt Bart trembling and knew he would not be able to contain his rising passion for long, nor her own. She undid his jacket and put her hands on his chest, feeling the warmth of his skin through the fine silk of his shirt.

'I've a confession to make about Rick,' she

told him quietly. 'Acting is one of my hobbies. That's how I came to play Rick's girl-friend.' Swiftly she recounted that part of the story. The rest Bart knew from San Francisco. 'I couldn't see any harm in it,' she ended, 'but then I didn't know I was going to meet you, and how that would complicate everything.'

Bart chuckled. 'Anything else to confess?'

'How much more can you take?' she teased.

'Whatever you give, sweetheart. One thing's for sure, *nothing*, but *nothing* you say will change my mind about marrying you.'

'For better, for worse, for richer, for poorer?' she teased.

'As far as I'm concerned you can give away every red cent your uncles left you—I think I might just manage to keep you without it!'

Melissa laughed. 'That's exactly what I've decided to do—but even then you won't be marrying a pauper. My parents left me a considerable sum—far more than I've ever needed, or wanted to spend.'

He pulled slightly away from her to look into her eyes, and she could see from his expression that he understood what she meant without her having to say it.

'So you also wanted to be loved for yourself alone?' he smiled. 'How lucky we are that we met each other!'

With a chuckle he began to kiss her again, soft, tender kisses all over her face before he came to her lips. Only then did passion appear, and his arms tightened their hold. Melissa's mouth parted beneath his and she pressed closer to him, and as he hardened against her,

her own desire began to supersede everything else.

'Aren't you tired after your journey?' she whispered. 'Don't you think you should go upstairs and lie down?'

'Are you trying to seduce me?' Bart asked with mock innocence.

She pushed him away, though still staying within the circle of his arms. 'Would you mind if I said yes?'

'Definitely not—I don't believe in playing hard to get!'

'Unlike me, that night at the villa!'

His mouth curled in reminiscence. 'I often wondered about that. Why *did* you change your mind?'

'Because I realised I was in love with you and was frightened going to bed with you would complicate things.'

'I can't pinpoint the exact moment I realised *I* loved *you*,' said Bart as they mounted the stairs, arms around each other's waists, 'though I wanted you from the beginning. Assuming you were Rick's girl clouded everything for me. But when I did finally understand what you meant to me, it made a mockery of everything I'd ever previously thought.'

Melissa thrilled to his words, words she'd longed to hear for so long.

'You seemed to forget I was Rick's girl when I was mugged,' she reminded him. 'I think that was the beginning.'

'Seeing you look so small and helpless brought out my paternal instincts!' he teased.

Her bedroom door closed behind them, and Melissa turned to face him.

'Who are you trying to kid, Bartholomew Reed Huntingdon the Fourth? There was never anything paternal about your instincts—they were always strictly lecherous!'

'And they still are.' Slowly he undid the buttons of her blouse and slipped it from her shoulders. 'We're going to spend the whole of our honeymoon in bed,' he said thickly. 'Perhaps, that way, when it's ended, I'll be able to concentrate on something other than you.'

Her skirt fell to the floor and she kicked it away with her foot. He looked at her standing supple before him, naked except for a single wisp of lace. His eyes darkened with desire and he drew her down on the bed. Only then did she reply.

'Don't rely on it, darling,' she whispered against his mouth. 'I intend the rest of our lifetime to be one *long* honeymoon!'

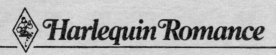

❖ Harlequin Romance

Coming Next Month

Available in January wherever paperback books are sold, or
through Harlequin Reader Service.

In the U.S.
901 Fuhrmann Blvd.
P.O. Box 1397
Buffalo, N.Y. 14240-1397

In Canada
P.O. Box 603
Fort Erie, Ontario
L2A 5X3

Coming Soon
from Harlequin...

GIFTS FROM THE HEART

**Watch for it
in February**